BAD BOYS
OVER EASY

BAD BOYS OVER EASY

Erin McCarthy
Jen Nicholas
Jordan Summers

BRAVA

KENSINGTON PUBLISHING CORP.
http://www.kensingtonbooks.com

BRAVA BOOKS are published by

Kensington Publishing Corp.
850 Third Avenue
New York, NY 10022

All Kensington titles, imprints and distributed lines are available at special quantity discounts for bulk purchases for sales promotion, premi-
ums, fund-raising, educational or institutional use.

Special book excerpts or customized printings can also be created to fit
specific needs. For details, write or phone the office of the Kensington
Special Sales Manager: Kensington Publishing Corp., 850 Third Avenue,
New York, NY 10022. Attn. Special Sales Department. Phone: 1-800-
221-2647.

Brava and the B logo Reg. U.S. Pat. & TM Off.

ISBN 0-7582-0845-6

First Kensington Trade Paperback Printing: April 2005
10 9 8 7 6 5 4 3 2 1

Printed in the United States of America

CONTENTS

Fuzzy Logic

Erin McCarthy

One

Lucas Manning was absolutely certain he hadn't ordered a box of neon pink dildos.

Yet there they were, packed four across, three deep in plastic bags, a faint rubbery smell rising from them. They were very bright. With sparkles.

"Holy crap."

Lucas closed the box back up to find the packing label. He hadn't actually looked to see who it was addressed to. The package had been sitting on the front porch outside his door and he'd brought it in the house with the rest of his mail.

He sure in the hell wished he'd looked first.

Or hadn't looked at all.

The box was addressed to Ashley Andrews, who lived in the upstairs apartment of his house. Ashley, his best friend Jason's older sister, who Lucas had secretly been lusting after for, oh, about the last decade.

And she had bought a case of dildos.

Lucas opened the box again and was sorry he had. They were so goddamn *pink*. And there were so many of them. What did one woman need all these for?

Since Lucas was a chemist and schooled in logic, he was

convinced there must be a logical explanation for this. He just had to figure out what it was. Leaving the box on his kitchen table, he went to the refrigerator for a beer.

He needed it to think.

So maybe Ashley had got up an order together with her friends so they could receive a group discount. That was kind of uninhibited, but plausible.

Maybe they were all for her, so one was always in easy reach. Lucas took a sip of his beer, swished it around his mouth. One for her bedroom, one for the living room, one for her purse . . . He stuck the cold bottle to his head. He was sweating.

One for the shower—damn, there was an image. Ashley, her wet blond hair clinging to her breasts, water sluicing down her fair skin, rocking onto a neon pink . . . He shifted uncomfortably from one foot to the other.

One for the kitchen? No, he just couldn't picture a sex toy alongside the spatulas. So that was only four. Which left eight unaccounted for. He tried to imagine other uses for them, but drew a blank. These were no cat toys.

Maybe she had ordered them online and had changed her order from one to two. Only when she had added the two, the one hadn't been removed and it had shown up as twelve. He could live with her buying two. Twelve was alarming.

Of course, Ashley's really good friend, Kindra, was getting married soon. Maybe these were gag gifts for the bachelorette party. That sounded reasonable. And Ashley liked to throw really fun parties.

Not that he'd ever been invited to any of them.

Ashley still thought of him as her little brother's geeky friend, Lucas.

Which, he supposed, was true.

But that didn't stop him from having a killer crush on her. She was so vibrant, so energetic, so enthusiastic that he got pleasure just from being near her.

But not twelve dildos' worth of pleasure.

Lucas set his beer bottle down with a hard slap. He picked up the box, grimacing.

Heading out onto the porch he took the two steps to Ashley's front door.

As he rang the bell he wondered if he should tape the box back up and plead ignorance.

Nah.

He'd never sleep again if he didn't hear the explanation for the package of pleasure addressed to her.

Ashley was a little astonished at what she'd do for money.

But she had gotten herself backed into a corner with her spending habits, and while her girlfriends were buying houses and taking nice vacations, Ashley had a closet full of expensive clothes and an empty checking account. Not to mention those credit card bills, which had crept from "Hmm, that's kind of high" to "Yikes!" level. Third World countries had less debt than she did.

It was time to get her finances back in the black.

The doorbell rang as she shifted the tickle-whip on her dining room table. Damn, she hoped no one was early for her debut as a Pleasure Party consultant. She didn't even have the lotions set out yet and the wine was still chilling.

The purple whip was clashing with the leopard print furry handcuffs. Grabbing it, she went to the door and threw it open, a smile pasted on her face.

Lucas was standing there holding a cardboard box. Her smile fell off her face and she sagged in relief. It was just Lucas, her little brother's friend, and her neighbor for the last two years. Fortunately, she had known Lucas since he had been in diapers and they had a deep affection for each other, like brothers and sisters.

Which meant she could rudely blow him off and it wouldn't matter.

"Oh, hey, Lucas, what's up?"

He shifted the box. "This was by my door, but it's yours. I opened it already thinking it was for me."

"That's okay." She grabbed the box from him and stuck it under her arm. "Thanks." She had every intention of slamming the door in his face, but he stepped forward.

"Ash?"

"Yeah?" She tossed her head, trying to get the hair out of her eyes without dropping the box or the tickle-whip.

Lucas had that look on his face, that serious, studying gaze that meant he was thinking hard. Sometimes she thought he looked cute when he was like that, sort of like a puppy dog sniffing out a bone. But it also reminded her that Lucas had more brainpower in one lobe than she had in her entire skull, and he always needed to understand everything. A curiosity that she just didn't have.

Not that they were kids anymore, and he wasn't following her around asking *why, why, why, Ashley*, but she had a party to put on and didn't have time for his theories on how they could improve energy efficiency in the house.

"Why are there twelve dildos in that box?"

Since she had expected something uber-intelligent to come out of his mouth, she just blinked for a second. Then shoved the whip in his hand so she could open the package. "Oh, they got here!"

Running her finger over the plastic bags, she said, "Cool! I didn't think they'd be here in time, which would have been a bummer. 'Pinky' is a top seller."

She was hoping to move at least three of these suckers tonight alone. It was possible, since she had over thirty people attending her open house to browse the Pleasure Party line of products, all designed to enhance your love life.

Trying to visualize where she could display one of them for her customers to see and touch and turn on, she moved to go back into her apartment, taking the steps to the second floor two at a time. Lucas was following her, she realized distractedly.

"Umm, Ashley . . ."

"What!" She dropped the box on the living room floor and surveyed her work so far. Using both her dining room and her living room, she had three tables lined up with products, from the handcuffs and a blindfold, to the full line of vibrators and toys. One table was empty, waiting for her to display the lotions and other edible products. She had interwoven strands of white Christmas lights among the products and used tulle and ribbons to dress displays up. It looked pretty darn good.

"You forgot this . . ." Lucas was waving the tickle-whip back and forth in the air, his caramel brown hair falling in his eyes the way it always did. He was wearing a white shirt and a blue striped tie with his khaki pants, looking like a J. Crew ad with his earnest look. All he needed was a blue blazer and the words *Feel* or something equally ridiculous slapped across his chest and he could be a teen model.

Of course, he wasn't really a teenager anymore. And when had he gotten those muscles in his forearms? Unnerved, Ashley frowned. What did she care if Lucas had started working out?

"You forgot this . . . what *is* this?"

Lucas knew what pi was and the theory of relativity, but she knew clothes and sex toys. Every woman needed a claim to fame.

"It's a tickle-whip. The feather end you use to, well, tickle." She grinned as his brown eyes enlarged. "And the other end you use to whip your partner without any risk of actual injury. Fun stuff, huh?" Not that she'd ever actually used one, but he didn't need to know that. It was just amusing to shock Lucas, who she suspected spent too much time at his computer.

Only he didn't look shocked.

"Really? Interesting." The whip end cracked into the palm of his hand. "Just enough sting, huh?"

Ashley jumped involuntarily. My God, was that lust in Lucas's eyes? Of course it wasn't. He was just interested, seeking all the answers, the way he always did. Next he'd be asking her the best way to use it for maximizing pleasure. Not because he wanted to use it, but because he wanted to know how everything worked. Pick it apart. Figure it out. Like the microwave he'd destroyed at age twelve.

"So, is there a reason your whole apartment is filled with sex toys? Or are you just entering a fun phase in your life?" He had the feather end under his chin now, rolling it back and forth so the purple plumes rose around him. He looked ridiculous.

And cute.

Damn it. Why was she thinking that? Flustered, Ashley ran her hand through her hair. "Put that down somewhere and help me unpack these lotions." If he was going to hang around, the least he could do was make himself useful. "And for your information, I'm trying to make some extra money so I'm selling romance enhancing products. I'm having an open house in an hour."

"Oh."

She could practically hear the wheels churning in his head at high speed.

"Have you personally tried all these products?"

The Pleasure Party company had seventy-three products in the line, two-thirds of them scattered around her apartment right now. Was he freaking serious? How much free time did he think she had?

"No." She was just going to leave it at that. If she volunteered any information, he'd be asking her which ones she'd tried and why.

"I wouldn't want to sell something I hadn't tried myself." Lucas had been studying a bottle of edible massage lotion. He opened it, squirted some on the back of his hand

and licked it. "Huh. Chocolate." His nose screwed up. "But somehow licking it off my own hand just doesn't do anything for me."

And before she could even protest, call him an idiot, or collect the twelve bucks retail that bottle cost, he reached out, snatched her arm and slathered chocolate lotion all over her.

But even stranger than that, was the sudden hot kick of interest from her inner thighs. Which was horrifying. She should be ashamed of herself.

Lucas was a *baby*.

Well, not that young exactly, since he was her brother Jason's age, and she was pretty sure Jason had turned twenty-five last December, but still. She was twenty-eight, damn near twenty-nine, she reminded herself firmly as his head bent over her.

Besides, she had never really thought of Lucas in a sexual way. He was too serious, too smart; he was above all those base physical urges.

He licked her arm.

Or not.

Two

Lucas hadn't meant to lick Ashley.

He wasn't usually impulsive, but he was curious if the lotion would taste different on her skin than it did on his. He imagined it was designed to react to an individual's body heat. Not to mention that everyone secreted different amounts of perspiration.

The opportunity to taste Ashley's flesh was too tempting to pass up.

So he had licked.

And damned if it didn't taste a hell of a lot better. In fact, it was delicious. Like rich, creamy, chocolate mousse, cool on a warm spoon.

"Mmm, that's good. Have you tried it?" Running his tongue over her moist wrist one more time to get the stray bits, Lucas chanced a glance up at Ashley.

Her green eyes were huge. Her breathing was a bit faster than normal. She shook her head, and Lucas had to acknowledge to himself that he was hopelessly, pathetically in love with her.

It was the only explanation for why he let her rent this apartment at half its market value, and why he could never seem to get involved with a woman beyond casual dating. It explained why he wanted to ram a fist into the face of every big stupid ugly jock Ashley had dated—and there had been quite a few.

He was in love with her, and just once he wanted her to see him as more than Jason's friend.

He wanted her to see him as a man.

Which was why he lifted her arm to her mouth. "Try it."

Ashley shook her head even harder. "No, I just ate dinner."

He nearly grinned, but kept it back. "It's not meant to fill you up, Ash, it's to turn you on."

She took a step back, yanking her arm from his grip, looking flustered. "Well, I know that. I'm the Pleasure Party consultant here, after all."

He was certain she'd make an excellent one. Ashley had good people skills, something he could not claim, and her enthusiasm could probably sell a hell of a lot of dildos. Yet she always seemed to underestimate herself, making comments about never being able to expect more than the entry-level job she had at a computer design firm.

It bothered him, which seemed to be further evidence that he was irrationally in love with her.

"What kind of training did you receive? For ease of selling, I would think you'd want to personally experience as many products as possible." His eye fell on the tickle-whip contraption he'd set down on the table. Had she used that?

On the one hand, the thought had him painfully hard. On the other hand, the idea that some guy—some low-IQ Encino Man, half a step below a chimp, bonehead used-car salesman—had taken a fake whip to Ashley's bare skin made him so angry the room sharpened into red-hot focus while his veins throbbed.

She wiped her wet arm on her pink-and-white striped skirt. It was soft and clingy and one side was shorter than the other. Her shirt was sleeveless, white, with a big fake pink flower pinned on it. It was kind of overblown and odd, but knowing Ashley, it was trendy and expensive. Her shoes were spiky little high-heeled sandals that looked painful at best, lethal at worst.

"Lucas, I don't have time for this. I'm not even finished setting up and people are going to be here in thirty minutes." She ripped open one "Pinky" and took it out of the package. Shaking it at him, she said, "Either help me unpack or go home."

He could honestly say that being reprimanded with a neon dildo was something of a strange experience. He felt like he had when he was thirteen and his dad had caught him with a pilfered *Playboy*. Ashamed and slightly dirty.

And fighting the urge to bust his gut laughing at the ridiculousness of it.

Lucas bent over and grabbed a box and hefted it onto the table. Ashley moved away from him, finding a spot for "Pinky" on another table, before she started fussing with some folders and brochures.

He arranged massage oils, lotions, and shaving cream onto the table in neat, tidy little rows. Looking at all the flavors and textures of lotions and powders, and reading all their buzz words like erogenous, erotic, maximum pleasure, and stimulate, he was getting a little uncomfortable.

"Is it hot in here? Is your air-conditioning unit working right?"

"Yes." Ashley had a rubber ducky in her hand.

"You sell rubber duckies? Isn't that kind of tame?"

She ripped the duck's head off. "It has a vibrating egg hidden inside." She pulled a small soft egg out and twisted it. It started humming. "It's a tub toy."

"Oh." He went back to his box, thinking. He didn't see the logic. "So, is it in a duck so no one knows it's there?"

"Yes."

"But . . . why would an adult have a toy duck? Wouldn't people think that was weird? And if you have kids in the house, wouldn't they want to play with it, and what if they accidentally unscrewed the head? Wouldn't that egg be a choking hazard?"

The look she shot him suggested she didn't know the answer. "Don't you have somewhere to be?"

She was trying to get rid of him, but he wasn't ready to leave just yet. It wasn't often he got a chance to see Ashley without her brother or without one of her best friends.

"No." He pulled out glow-in-the-dark condoms from the box.

"So, what's the point in these?" He spoke half to himself, genuinely puzzled. "I mean, they don't glow until they're out of the package, so it can't be meant to lead you to the nightstand. And the man is the one who needs air traffic control guiding him in, not the woman. In fact, I would think seeing a glowing pink penis would scare the shit out of most women, wouldn't it?"

"I'm assuming that's a rhetorical question." Ashley disappeared into the kitchen.

"Well, have you used these?"

"No." Her voice carried loudly and vehemently.

Products all arranged to his satisfaction, he tucked the empty box under the table and started browsing. "Why would anyone want edible underwear?" He shook the box and sniffed it. "I mean, it's not like you'd wear them all day. You would only put them on in the heat of the moment, and wouldn't that sort of kill the spontaneity of the whole thing? Like here, go put these on so I can eat them off . . . and how can these possibly be one size fits all? That doesn't make any sense."

Ashley came clicking back into the room and slapped a cheese and crackers tray down on the coffee table. "Lucas Manning, some things don't make sense, all right? They just don't. People do them because they're fun. F-U-N. Fun. Got it? Because it's silly and sexy and exciting to do something crazy and maybe even stupid when you're attracted to someone. Can you understand that?"

Oh, hell yeah, he could understand that. Because he was attracted to her and about to do something crazy and even stupid.

"So if I pulled up your shirt and smeared this peach powder across your nipples, it would be fun?"

Ashley closed her eyes for a split second. Oh, Lord, help her. He was so smart, yet so damn dumb when it came to common sense. He had no idea that you couldn't just run around discussing touching a woman's nipples and not expect them to harden. Like hers just had.

Which was ridiculous. Lucas was talking about her nipples in a purely scientific manner. He was trying to understand the logic behind romance enhancing products, and she was pretty sure there just wasn't any. And in the meantime, he had somehow managed to arouse her.

It must be all the aphrodisiacs in the room. The power of suggestion. It couldn't possibly have anything to do with Lucas, whose smiles were so infrequent as to attract notice, and whose hair looked like he'd forgotten to comb it for a week solid. But in all fairness, Lucas was a very good-looking guy. Who suddenly when she wasn't looking had sprouted to over six feet tall and broadened out a bit.

"In theory, yes, that would be fun, given the right circumstances." She put a hand on her stomach, as if she could press the alarming heat out of her womb.

"What would those circumstances be?"

She barely heard the question, frozen in place watching him unscrew the lid on the jar and pull out the little feather duster applicator. "Well, it would be if two people were settling in for a night of making love. I don't think you'd want to rush through this kind of foreplay."

His brown eyes pierced hers in concentration as he closed the two feet between them. "So, you wouldn't want to just smear it on the nipples then? You'd want to start maybe with the shoulder."

The brush touched her skin and she shivered. He moved

it gently back and forth over her shoulder while she tried to find the willpower to step away. But before she could even think to react, his tongue was on her, sliding in little swirls around and around before his mouth dropped down completely over her in a wet embrace and he sucked.

She almost fell off her stilettos she was so shocked. "Lucas!"

"No, the shoulder isn't right?" The feather dabbed her neck, close to her collarbone. "Maybe here, then?"

And dang it if he didn't start licking and sucking there too, until she was curling her toes and fisting her hands and tilting her head back. He didn't touch her anywhere else, and her body started to strum and hum and ache for attention.

Which was just so wrong. This was *Lucas*. He had seen her with braces and acne and bad hair. This was Lucas, who she loved absolutely, in a pure sisterly sort of way. She'd do anything for Lucas.

Apparently even let him experiment with her body for the sake of sexual science.

A shaky sigh fell out of her mouth before she could stop it.

Maybe this was ecstasy envy. She hadn't had sex in eight months, since her last boyfriend had moved to Chicago for a better job opportunity. He hadn't suggested they keep in touch and she hadn't been all that broken up. Chad wasn't the brightest bulb in the pack and his jokes had become wearing after a while.

Not that she wanted to date someone smart, like a genius, who would make her feel inadequate, like she had her whole life, growing up with a super-intelligent brother. But she didn't want to date someone dumb either. She'd settle for a happy medium.

Since Kindra was engaged and her friend Violet was seriously dating someone, she knew they were both getting it on a regular basis. Maybe this bizarre arousal was just her body's way of reminding her that she was heading into her peak sexual years and this wasn't the time to neglect it.

Lucas dusted powder on her chin and sucked. She grabbed his arms for balance and tried not to be turned on. His whiskers rubbed against her cheek and his hair tickled her nose and his tongue started shifting upward and, damn, she was turned on.

Especially when his finger tapped her bottom lip, depositing powder on it. The peachy fragrance drifted up to her nostrils, and without thinking her tongue darted out and licked a tiny bit. It melted in her mouth in a juicy sweet river.

"No, I'm supposed to taste it," Lucas murmured against the corner of her mouth.

Then he was rolling his tongue across her moist lip, clear from one side to the other, making little sounds of approval at the taste. Ashley's fingers curled tighter in his shirtsleeves and her breath jerked out of her in little ragged bursts.

She wasn't sure what was happening, wasn't sure why she was letting Lucas lap at her like a dog with a bowl of water, but oh my, it felt so good, and no matter how loud her brain screamed, her feet weren't walking her away.

Suddenly he shifted, and he was kissing her. Just plain and simple kissing her, his lips locked over hers and his tongue doing reconnaissance in her mouth. The sweet peachy powder still clung to both of their tongues and the embrace was hot, wet, exciting, full of heat and passion.

When Lucas finally pulled back, she heard a great lusty sigh emerge from her own mouth. Lucas's eyes were dark, half closed, his lips shiny. But he simply said, "The peach is definitely better than the chocolate."

Ashley relinquished her death hold on his shirt and tried to take a step back. She hit the table with her backside, wobbling on her stilettos and upsetting the display of disco vibrators. Whirling around, she placed the yellow, blue, and red vibrators with flashing chaser lights back to the original position. Her cheeks were flushed and hot.

"So I should push the peach then?" she managed, hoping her voice didn't warble.

Here Lucas had just been curious, like he always was, and she had gone all weak in the knees and wet in her panties.

"Definitely."

Then she could hear packaging tearing and she was forced to turn around in exasperation. "What are you opening now? This stuff was expensive."

"But you need some things opened for demos, right? More customers will buy if they can taste, touch, and try the product. These lotions are perfect for that." He held up a little jar he'd pulled out of the box. "This stuff is supposed to heat your skin and tingle."

If he tried to pull up her shirt and touch her nipple with that crap, she was going to scream. He was starting to unnerve her. Maybe he was so elevated intellectually that he could isolate his brain from his penis, but she wasn't on quite such a higher plane. He was making her horny.

Since he had no intention of having sex with her and she had no intention of having sex with her little brother's best friend, at the end of the night he was going to leave her hot and aroused, with no one but rubber ducky for company.

And no matter how naughty and inventive the Pleasure Party ducky was, nothing beat a real man covering you.

"And your samplers can be for personal use as well then."

Lucas reached out for her and she yelled, "Don't!"

But he was only turning her wrist over and rubbing the cream into the soft skin at the bottom of her palm. "Don't what?"

"Uh . . . don't get it on my skirt, please." She was aware that sounded lame, but her brain had stopped working.

Never in her entire life had she suspected her wrist could be sexy.

But the way Lucas was stroking it with the pad of his thumb, in little floating circles, was oddly, incredibly sensual.

"Is it getting hot? Tingling?"

"Yes. Very hot. Everything is hot and tingling," she whispered.

All over every part of her she was hot and tingling and starting to think something was wrong with her, and damn, damn, was he going to kiss her again?

His body moved closer to hers.

The doorbell rang. Ashley jumped back two feet. "Oh, shit, someone's here!"

But she was secretly relieved, even if her show wasn't completely set up yet.

Another split second and she might have been doing some serious cradle robbing.

Three

Lucas watched Ashley bolt down the stairs like her skirt was on fire.

He knew the feeling. His pants felt capable of melting steel—twenty-five hundred degrees Fahrenheit was all that was needed, and he was certain he had achieved it.

Oh, man, he sure hoped he knew what the hell he was doing here. He didn't want to ruin his relationship with Ashley, but he couldn't stand by any longer and pretend he didn't care about her in a way that wasn't even remotely brotherly.

If he tried to tell her his feelings and she rejected him, well, hopefully it wouldn't affect their friendship. But this way—this waiting, this wanting, this ache—he couldn't live like this. He had to know if there was any chance, however remote, that Ashley might be attracted to him in return.

So far, she looked a little confused. But she wasn't balking at his overtures either.

And if he wasn't mistaken, she had enjoyed that kiss.

The feeling was mutual. Tasting her tongue had about seared his clothes right off his body.

Ashley came back up the stairs, her heels clicking on the

hardwood floors. Her friend Kindra was with her, wearing shorts and a tank top, her auburn hair back in a ponytail.

"Oh, hey, Lucas."

"Hi, Kindra. How's it going?"

"Good." Kindra set her purse down on the floor. "Except I'm so ready for my wedding to be over. Just done and over. My advice to everyone and anyone is to skip the wedding and elope." She glanced at the tables of products. "But I also figure if Mack and I can survive planning this wedding from hell without killing each other, then we can make it through anything."

"Well, I hope it all goes well for you." Lucas put the lid back on the peach powder and returned the jar to its box. He was tempted to take it home with him, but it didn't make sense to remove it from the source of its true entice-ment—Ashley.

Ashley got him hot, not the powder.

"Are you staying for the party, Lucas?" Kindra asked.

"No!" Ashley said, horror in her voice. Then she tucked her blond curls behind her ear and cleared her throat. "Men can't be at these parties. It's company policy."

"That's logical," Kindra said. "Otherwise it could have the potential to dissolve into an orgy."

Lucas tried to picture it, but couldn't. "Your friends must be more exciting than mine."

Kindra laughed.

"Lucas was helping me set up, but now he's leaving. Right, Lucas?" Ashley gave him a bright smile, a warning in her eyes.

He stared back. "Right. I'll get out of your hair. But I'm coming back after the party to do some shopping. There are a few things I'd like to try—hands-on."

Ashley's jaw dropped. Then she glanced at Kindra, who wasn't even really listening to them. She was fingering a black silk blindfold.

"Lucas has this need to know how everything works. Bikes, microwaves, edible underwear—" Ashley broke off, her hand on her chest. Her cheeks were stained pink.

She was blushing. And babbling. Lucas figured that was a good sign. If she wasn't interested in him at all, she would have just told him to knock it off and taken the lotion away from him.

Instead, she looked confused.

"I'll see you later then. I'll give you a call to make sure everyone has left." He started for the stairs.

"Okay."

Lucas shot a long lingering look at that purple ticklewhip as he walked by it. He could really, really see the appeal in that. Brushing that feather over Ashley's breasts . . . he glanced back at her over his shoulder.

He definitely had the need to see how that worked.

Ashley broke out in a sweat.

Holy smokes, Lucas had just checked out the ticklewhip. She was sure of it. He had stared at it, then at her. Like he was picturing using it.

On her.

Oh, my.

She didn't move until the front door downstairs slammed shut, then she collapsed on her bright blue sofa. There was sweat on her inner thighs. *Sweat* on her goddamn inner thighs. Maybe her air-conditioning was broken.

"Is it hot in here, Kindra?"

"No." Kindra shook the box of edible underwear then put it back down. "Unless you count the sexual tension between you and Lucas. That was hot enough to melt chocolate."

Ashley fanned herself. "There is no sexual tension between Lucas and me! He's my little brother's best friend. My little brother, who is a genius, by the way. And Lucas is his genius friend. Who is only twenty-five years old. Way too young for me, way too smart for me, even if I were interested, which I'm not."

She was protesting too much. She knew it and winced.

Kindra raised an eyebrow. "Oh, you poor thing. Suffering from sexual tension *and* delusions."

Was she? She certainly felt delusional. Like she had dreamed that erotic kiss they had shared.

"Just a little friendly advice . . . why don't you just go for it? You like Lucas, don't you?"

"As a person, yes, of course I do. We grew up together. He's a very sweet, honest guy. I love him like a brother." Which made her current feelings sick and incestuous.

"Maybe there's more to those feelings than that. You're not the kind to just sleep with a guy for the heck of it, and Lucas doesn't seem like the kind of guy to do that either. So maybe there's something really there and you should explore it." Kindra picked up a vibrator and waved it around. "I don't think Lucas is really all that interested in sex toys. I think he's interested in you. That's why he's coming back here tonight."

Oh, damn, he was coming back, wasn't he. She honestly wasn't sure how she felt about that. "You know, the problem with your friends getting married is that they suddenly think they know everything about relationships. Just because you and Mack are happy nesting in your house with your poodle doesn't mean the rest of us are looking for that."

Kindra laughed. "That may be true. But if love and marriage were there, you wouldn't say no to them, would you?"

No, she supposed she wouldn't. But the thought of love and marriage at all, let alone in relation to Lucas—well, it gave her hives. She literally itched and ached to get out of her own skin.

"And you can't tell me you aren't completely preoccupied thinking about Lucas, because you haven't even once mentioned how you hate my outfit, which is usually the first thing you say when you see me."

Well, now that Kindra mentioned it. "Those shorts do look kind of outdated, Kindra. They go practically to your knees."

"My fiancé doesn't seem to mind my clothes." She grinned. "Though truthfully, he prefers me in no clothes at all. And given the look on Lucas's face, I bet he would love to see you naked."

The doorbell rang. Ashley stood up, relieved to escape any conversation that mentioned love, nudity, and Lucas in the same sentence. "Sometimes it's better to leave things a mystery."

Kindra cleared her throat, a smile on her face. "And sometimes the real thing, with a man who adores you, is better than any sex toy could ever be."

Ashley couldn't dispute that. "I'm not arguing with you Kindra, but before I can even consider falling in love and start planning my own wedding from hell, I need to sell some sex toys and get my credit card debt down into the single digits. And even if I did fall in love and get married, it wouldn't be with Lucas."

She didn't think. It would be highly unlikely. Even if she did already love Lucas, it wasn't *love*. Or was it?

The thought had her rushing down the stairs too quickly, stumbling, and nearly breaking her neck before she skidded to a stop at the front door. She threw the door open. "Hi! Thank you so much for coming."

The next ten minutes were spent answering the door and giving greetings. Then Ashley was knee-deep in her demos, passing lotions and candles around for her friends to smell.

It should have been enough of a distraction to turn her mind from Lucas. Instead, it only made it worse. With every laugh, every bawdy remark someone made, every product she picked up, she thought about Lucas and his strange, arousing behavior.

It didn't help that her brother Jason's girlfriend, Hope, was there, showing an incredibly inappropriate amount of interest in every single item. *Hello. Boyfriend's sister here.* Didn't Hope know that she was getting all sorts of gross mental images?

Of course she had invited the girl, but she had just thought Hope would come along and buy some shaving cream out of charity. Her brother's girlfriend was a medical student, aspiring to be a surgeon. She wore glasses. She wasn't supposed to be coveting a book on sexual positions.

Ashley's friend Trish was glancing through the book with Hope. "Ooh, that's a good one."

"Done it already," Hope said.

"No kidding?" Respect crept into Trish's voice.

Bile rose in Ashley's mouth. She turned and grabbed her glass of wine.

"It's the scientist in Jason," Hope continued. "He likes to try and defy gravity."

Eeew! She so did not want to know that about her brother. And God, did that mean Lucas would be the same way? Huh. Now that was kind of sexy.

"So he just has to hold on here with his . . ."

"Hope!" Ashley blurted out. "TMI—too much information! Come on, this is my little brother you're talking about."

Hope blinked those innocent looking brown eyes behind her owlish glasses. She giggled. "Oh, sorry, Ash."

Her cousin Jenny stopped sniffing the strawberry edible lotion to demand, "Bring out the vibrators and stuff, Ashley. We want to get to the good stuff."

Pasting a smile on her face, Ashley held up Pinky and gave her little rehearsed speech about his many features, including being waterproof. All of her guests had wish lists she'd passed around, so they could write down the names of products that they were interested in as they came around.

Everyone started writing after viewing Pinky, except for Trish and their friend Violet, who looked speechless.

"Aren't you going to write this one down?" Hope asked Violet. "It looks like a good one, and that's a great price."

Violet just swallowed hard and shook her head. "I don't think I would even know what to do with that."

Ashley laughed, though she had a feeling Violet wasn't kidding. She'd seen Violet's latest boyfriend. Sweet, but a total geek. Which about summed up all of Violet's boyfriends.

Hope turned to Trish. "Well, what about you? Didn't you like this one?"

Ashley took a gander at Hope's wineglass. Empty. It figured. She had a strong feeling Hope was drunk. At least she hoped she was, or Ashley was going to have a little chat with Jason.

"I don't do vibrators or dildos or whatever you want to call them."

"Why not?" Hope looked genuinely puzzled.

Trish stuck her pencil behind her ear, where it jutted through her short hair. "Because you all have boyfriends and it's okay to play around with stuff like that. I'm single. So if I get a vibrator, that's all I've got going on. And I don't want to become dildo dependent."

The room erupted with laughter. Ashley snorted before she clapped her hand over her mouth. "Dildo dependent?"

"Yes, I've heard women get so dependent on their vibrators, that they can't have orgasms without them. They have to wean themselves off the machinery. I just don't want to go there."

Three people scratched Pinky off their lists.

Ashley glared at Trish. She could see her point, but she was trying to make a quick buck here. She was going to pay her bills off and reform. She was going to stop buying clothes beyond her means. But first she needed to push some product.

Trish gave her a sheepish look and mouthed *sorry*. Then her voice rose enthusiastically. "But I'm definitely buying those colored condoms. A single woman always needs to have condoms on hand."

Violet patted Trish's leg. "Nice save."

Ashley was starting to think she was learning way more than she ever wanted to know about her friends' and her family's sex lives.

Four

Lucas peered through his blinds at the street. It looked like the last of the cars crowding their driveway and the front of the house had pulled away. The wild eruptions of laughter and loud female shoes traipsing back and forth above his head had stopped. The front door slamming over and over had quieted.

He was almost positive Ashley was alone.

And he was tired of waiting.

Watching TV and playing computer solitaire had done nothing to curb his desire for Ashley. If anything, the three hours spent in itchy anticipation had made him more eager than before. And sweaty.

Standing on top of the central air-conditioning vent to cool himself off, he called Ashley's apartment.

"Hello?" she said breathlessly after four rings.

Lucas swallowed hard, and shifted so the cold air would shoot straight up his boxer shorts. "It's me. Everybody leave?"

"Yes."

"Can I come up?" He held his breath, eyes closed.

"Sure."

Thank you. Lucas strove to sound nonchalant instead of desperate. "Cool. I'll be up in a second."

"The door's open."

He hung up the phone, ran across his apartment in a fast sprint, and turned his shower on cold. He stripped off his boxers and took a thirty-second shower to remove the stickiness from his skin and to shrink his erection. He didn't want to lay all his cards on the table when he walked in, so to speak, and a big old boner would be doing just that.

Two minutes later he was locking his front door, his hair hanging wet over his forehead. He stuck his keys in his jeans pocket and looked at the bottle of beer in his hand. He'd picked it up for a swallow on his way past the coffee table and had forgotten to set it down. Oh, well. He wasn't taking an extra three seconds to return it.

Nor was he wearing shoes or a shirt. It was a hot, muggy July night and he was horny. He didn't need additional clothes to sweat through.

Ashley's front door was unlocked like she'd said, probably from all her friends leaving. He shot the dead bolt behind him, even though they lived in a safe neighborhood. He didn't like the idea of her being unprotected even for five minutes. It was why he'd given her the upstairs apartment, since it was less likely someone would go in through the windows on the second floor.

Lucas kept an eye on Ashley, whether she realized it or not. And he would continue to do that, no matter what the outcome of this night was.

When he got to the top of the stairs, he saw her back, bent over a box, packing something into it. She had taken her shoes off and her blond hair tumbled wildly down her tank top. It was sexy hair, curly and riotous, going every which way with a mind of its own. He wanted to know what it would look like brushing over her naked flesh instead of white cotton.

"Hey, Ashley." He put his beer to his mouth and took a long pull.

Ashley had heard Lucas come up the stairs, but she waited for him to speak before acknowledging him, feeling weirdly nervous. But when she turned, she wished like hell that she had just caught his eye as he came up the stairs, and given him a friendly wave.

Because she wasn't prepared for what she saw.

Lucas was standing in the door frame, wearing nothing but soft, faded jeans slipping low on his hips. He was barefoot. Bare-chested.

The last time she'd really stopped and taken a gander at Lucas, she was pretty darn sure he hadn't sported a chest like that. All firm and strong and grown-up sexy.

With his damp hair clinging to his forehead and his bicep flexing as he lifted a beer to his lips and drank, he no longer reminded her of a teen model. He looked like a beer commercial, a cigarette ad, an underwear billboard. The perfect masculine image that had first tripped into her consciousness when she was about thirteen and had realized there was something in between scrawny middle school boys and her father's soft paunch.

In between was this.

And it was gorgeous.

"Hi," she said, dropping the Ben-Wa balls she'd been holding.

"Do you need help cleaning up?" He set his beer down on her coffee table and walked toward her.

"No, I guess not. I just need to throw this stuff in boxes and stick it in the closet. I haven't really figured out how to organize it yet."

"Don't put it all away yet. I want to check some of it out."

That's what she was afraid of. "Maybe another time, Lucas, when I'm not so tired, okay?" After she had time to think about the fact that she could be attracted to Lucas. After she'd had time to convince herself that she wasn't.

"It's hard work selling sex toys, huh?" He sat on the couch and patted the seat next to him. "Take a load off, Ash. You've been walking around all night in those heels; your feet must be killing you. I'll pack all the boxes up for you."

She wasn't sure why, but she sat down next to him. Her shoulders screamed as she relaxed them. "The crowd control is the toughest part, I found out. You have to keep them focused on what you're selling, but people get silly because it's fun and sexy and sometimes a little embarrassing. I want the women to laugh and have fun, but I don't want the party to last five hours either, you know?"

"Were the sales good?" Lucas turned on the couch, his hand snaking up to her neck.

Ashley started a little at the feel of his fingers on her bare skin, but when he began rubbing her sore muscles, she sighed. "Yes, actually, I profited five hundred bucks tonight."

"Really? That's a lot of edible underwear." Lucas sounded fascinated.

"But I'm not sure I thought this whole thing through. I invested two grand up front on all these products, and I made fifty percent of the retail price as profit, but I have to reorder to replace what I've sold, so it will take four parties like tonight just to break even." She was getting a headache just thinking about it. "Sometimes I think I'm lacking in a financial commonsense gene. I touch money and it disappears. I'm an idiot when it comes to money management."

The balance on her credit card flashed in her head like a humiliating score card. *Ashley The Idiot's Team Take-home pay is negative fifteen grand after taxes, rent, and all of her stupid mistakes.* "I'm worse than that. I'm a financial fuck-up."

"Come on. Don't be so hard on yourself. In the grand

scheme of mistakes, this one's not so bad. Not like joining a gang and embarking on a crime spree."

Ashley laughed. "No, that's not really me."

"This is fixable. Three more parties like tonight and you break even. Three more after that and you pocket fifteen hundred bucks. That's not bad for something like fifteen hours of work. And you're a damn good salesperson. You're knowledgeable about your products and enthusiastic." Lucas stopped rubbing her neck and dropped his arm. "I bet you could sell me anything on that table. Come on."

He stood up and grabbed her hand. "Sell me something, Ash."

"Lucas . . ." she protested, but she couldn't help but smile as he tugged on her arm. He was being awfully sweet.

So she let him pull her to her feet. Then she grinned when he picked up the box with the Ben-Wa balls.

"What does this do?"

"Those are multipurpose metal balls. They can help develop stronger muscles, like Kegel exercises do, but in a way that's much more fun. And they can also aid in sexual stimulation, either alone or with your partner."

She pressed her lips together to prevent laughter as Lucas frowned, his eyebrows drawing in. He wasn't getting it.

"But . . . what . . ."

"You insert them in the vagina."

"Really?" His expression made her laugh outright. He gingerly set the box back down.

"Okay, well, you can sell me anything but those."

Just to tease, she said, "But you said I could sell anything. I guess I'm not that great, after all."

"No, no, anything else. Come on." He picked up the black satin blindfold. "Okay, here, what's this?"

She snorted. "It's a blindfold, obviously. For titillating foreplay. Or if you're single, consider it a beauty mask, or a way to shield that bright morning sun on Saturdays."

"I could use that. There, sold." He set the blindfold aside. "See? You're great at this. What else?"

"How about some fur-lined handcuffs? Feel how soft they are." Ashley rubbed the fabric across his wrists. She was amused at Lucas, pleased that he cared enough to try so hard to make her feel better. She was actually starting to have fun with this.

"Very nice. Definitely got to have those." He took the cuffs from her and set them on the blindfold. "And I can tell you right now I want one of those tickle-whips."

He locked eyes with her. She gulped. "Do you now?"

"Oh, yeah." Lucas's expression was unreadable, but his eyes burned into her, his body leaned toward her, his arms reaching, reaching . . . He snatched up a box, brushing his forearm across her breasts.

She sucked in her breath. Any doubts she had about her attraction to him evaporated. She wanted Lucas, plain and simple, for whatever reason. Her body was hot, heavy, her inner thighs wet, a knot of desire growing in her belly.

"What's this?"

Focusing on what he held up, she tucked her hair behind her ear, and strove for nonchalant. "Umm, that's a, uh, cock ring." She had been practicing saying that word out loud in her apartment, so she wouldn't giggle when she had to say it at her parties. But she still stammered, especially since she had a sudden inexplicable interest in that word in relation to Lucas.

Yet it wasn't an embarrassed stammer, but a husky, interested tumble over her words that made her blush deeper than saying cock ring.

"A what?" Lucas turned the blue jelly ring around in his hand. "I never felt the need to decorate mine, but maybe that's just me."

Ashley wanted to laugh, but was too aroused to do more than let out a soft sound of amusement. She put her hand next to his on the ring, intending to pull it away from him.

But he stroked her skin, effectively holding her hand, and she froze, blurting out her rehearsed speech. "Actually, it's meant to help sustain an erection, for both you and your partner's increased pleasure."

Her arm was brushing across the bare flesh of his hard stomach and she stood completely and utterly still, afraid to move, afraid of what he might do. Afraid of what she might do.

"I see," he whispered, his voice low, gravelly, raw.

She wondered what he would say next. Obviously he wasn't really going to buy any of these things, but she was curious if pride would make him say no or if he would go along with the idea.

"Well. If it's for my woman's pleasure, then of course, I'll have to get it."

His gaze swept over her lips, her breasts, and Ashley thought that was the sexiest thing she'd ever heard any man say.

Five

While Lucas was aware that he had just admitted in a roundabout way that he needed help keeping it up for long periods of time, he didn't care. Ashley seemed to need a confidence boost, and he'd say anything, even claim he was a virgin if it would make her feel better.

That might actually be a good plan. He could ask her to show him how to use all these products.

But he wasn't that desperate yet. He still had hopes that Ashley was intrigued by him. That she was seeing him differently tonight for the first time.

"Don't forget I want the peachy powder stuff too," he told her. "So what's my total so far?" He'd probably spent a hundred bucks already.

She let go of the cock ring with a jerk. Lucas couldn't believe he was actually going to have to take that thing home. Maybe he could freeze it and use it in his lunches. Keep his turkey sandwich cold.

"Let me get my calculator." She shot him a questioning, sideways glance. "You don't really want this stuff, do you?"

"Of course I do."

Her look turned mischievous. "Are you sure you don't

want the Ben-Wa balls then? It could be a sexy surprise for your girlfriend."

"I don't have a girlfriend." Tucking his hands in his back pockets, he studied her. "But I'm working on it."

She knew he meant her. He could see it in the way her eyes widened and her mouth fell open.

"You like Ben-Wa balls, Ash?" He picked the box up, never breaking eye contact. "Add these to my bill." Reaching out, he opened her fingers, set the balls in her hand. "Consider it a gift."

Just the thought of her in her bed, naked, rolling those little things up inside her had him harder than hell.

Her tongue moved out and moistened her rosy bottom lip. Her fingers closed around the box of balls.

What came from her mouth next would probably determine the course of the night, maybe even the course of their relationship from here on out.

So when she paused, he decided to add some additional persuasion.

He kissed her. One hand wrapped over hers, the other rising to her cheek, he tasted her deep, with no pretense of licking peach powder off her.

Just with all his feelings, all his desire for her, all his love.

She opened for him without hesitation.

His control started to fragment as he took it deeper, wilder, his tongue plunging in to meet hers, Ashley's fingers splaying across his chest. She tasted good, felt so wonderful in his arms, and he shifted his leg to get nearer to her.

But she pulled back, and their excited breathing filled the room. Through puffy, shiny lips, she said, "What are we doing, Lucas?"

"We're doing what I've wanted to for a long time." He ran a finger across her jaw.

"I thought you were just curious about all these sex toys. That you were trying to figure out their use and purpose."

"While I am curious how all this stuff works, I came up here tonight because I want you, not a sex toy."

She looked worried. "Define want."

Lucas kissed her jaw, trailed his lips up to her earlobe and nibbled on it. "I want to make love to you. I want to give you pleasure." He also wanted to love her, marry her, have children with her, but that much information might scare her. As it was, she looked like a strong wind could knock her over.

Her head tilted back, and when he dipped his tongue into her ear, she moaned. "How old are you?"

The question was unexpected, but he answered automatically, more interested in the graceful line from her neck to her shoulder. "Twenty-five."

"When's your birthday? It's in April, isn't it?"

"April seventeenth." He shifted so his thighs closed around hers and her belly pressed enticingly into his erection.

"So you're just barely twenty-five."

"I guess." Her breasts rested against his bare chest, and he reveled in the sensation.

"You're too young for me." She pushed against him like she wanted out of his arms.

Lucas looked up at her. Was she serious? "I'm an adult, Ash. I know what I want. And three years doesn't mean a damn thing."

"It doesn't?" She was relaxing again. "It seems like it should."

"It doesn't," he quickly assured her and cupped her breast, closing his eyes briefly at the sensation of her heavy in his hand.

"Oh damn, that feels good." She squirmed a little. "But we still shouldn't do this."

"Why not?" He stroked over her nipple, wrenching a gasp from her.

"We're friends, we've always been friends, and I don't want to ruin that." Biting her lip, she sighed. "But wow, I am so attracted to you right now."

"The feeling is mutual." He kissed her forehead. "If you want me to go back downstairs, I will. But I don't want to."

Ashley felt like one of the problems with her personality was that she was too impulsive. She didn't think things through.

She was trying to make better choices, weigh the pros and cons before just jumping into something.

But her mind was mush. Cold, runny, leftover mush. She couldn't think about anything rational when Lucas was stroking her nipple and moving his lip back and forth on her forehead.

All her brain could seem to focus on was that she wanted Lucas to make love to her. She really, really wanted him to, in a way she couldn't remember ever wanting another man.

She cared about him, she trusted him completely, and when she looked into his eyes, she saw something she didn't understand, but that made her feel she was just about the most desirable woman in the world.

So she opened her mouth and told him, "Don't go. I want you to stay."

Damn, she couldn't believe she'd just said that.

But Lucas leaned back so she could see his face. Then he gave her the most beautiful smile she'd ever seen on him, one that lifted sweetly, a little crooked, and went all the way up to his eyes. It did strange things to her insides and left her breathless.

"Ashley."

He gave her a light kiss, a feathering of his lips over hers, so that she barely had a taste of him, barely got to feel him against her before he was gone. It was a caring kiss, not a passionate kiss, and it sent her deeper into confusion, panic, concern that she was acting on a hormonal impulse and would live to regret it.

Oh, well. She was sure she'd done stupider things, and he was doing the most delightful things to the underside of her breasts. Somehow when she hadn't been looking or thinking or noticing anything but the desire in his eyes, he had worked her tank top up to her bra.

Now his fingers were stroking back and forth, slowly, steadily, enticingly, on her bare skin below her bra. Jumping up from time to time to tease her nipple with a barely-there touch.

She'd never thought of herself as a passive lover, but this was different. Lucas was different. She knew him, but she'd never seen him like this, with this lusty determination on his face. It had her aroused, yet unsure of her own role. So she just stood there and let him touch, let him take the lead.

Which he was. He seemed to be approaching her the same way he would a chemical equation. He was assessing her, observing her reactions, deciding on the best plan to proceed with. He was slow and steady, lips on her neck, her shoulder, nuzzling, caressing, while his fingers touched higher and higher until they were brushing back and forth over her nipples.

Ashley swallowed hard, her legs quivering, her pulse racing. She was still clutching the Ben-Wa balls in her hand, and suddenly aware of the fact, she reached back for the table, intent on dumping them. The image of those balls, what he could do with them, was so hot and scorching she nearly moaned. Too much. It was all too much to take in.

His eyes followed her movement. "Maybe later," he whispered, his mouth rubbing over the front of her shirt, right at the swell of her breast. "The second or the third time."

He yanked the cup of her bra down at the same second she realized his meaning. Ashley sucked in her breath. He meant more than once, tonight. He meant all night. He meant . . . oh, boy.

"Sounds like you've got this all figured out."

With one expert flick, he popped open her bra. Why had she ever stupidly thought that Lucas was naïve when it came to women? He clearly knew his way around intimate apparel.

"I've had a lot of time to think about it, and what I want."

He took a step back, and she whimpered when his hands fell off her.

"And right now I want to see you naked. And then I'm going to touch and taste every inch of you."

If he insisted.

Six

Lucas was having a hard time not just ripping Ashley's clothes off and taking her on the Pleasure Party table.

But he had meant what he'd said. He had anticipated this moment for years, never really expecting it could actually happen, and he wanted to savor it. Savor her. Savor the feeling that he could give Ashley pleasure.

"Well, that's getting right to the point, isn't it?" She smiled at him then, a naughty suggestive smile that made his gut clench and his groin tighten.

Ashley had been tense a minute before, but now she seemed to have made a decision to enjoy this shift in their relationship.

"Are you going to get me naked or should I?" Her tongue slipped out and wet her bottom lip.

She looked gorgeous with her flushed cheeks and her wild curls, with her shirt shoved up and the top of one breast peeking out of her unhooked bra. She had golden skin, and a tiny silver ring in her belly button above her skirt that made him want to lick it.

No woman was as attractive to him as Ashley was, because she was a beautiful woman and because he was in love with her. And one way or another, tonight she was going to be his.

"Oh, I'm going to get you naked." He tossed his hair out of his eyes. "If you don't mind."

She shook her head. "I don't mind."

Lucas's heart filled. Damn, this was everything he wanted, everything he could ever hope for. Ashley in front of him, desire in her eyes, and a sweet smile playing about her lips. Did she even know what she meant to him? He wanted to tell her, knew he shouldn't.

So he reached for her and took the shirt over her head, her hair tumbling back over her shoulders as the tank top cleared her head. He dropped it onto the empty box Ashley had set on the table to pack up her products.

Since her bra was sliding down her arms and was crooked on her breasts, he just pulled down the straps and flung it over in the direction of the shirt. Then stopped to look. To stare. To mentally groan and to try not to grovel.

Damn. His blood rushed, his pulse pounded, and his jeans were unbearably tight.

"Stop looking at me like that." Ashley was blushing, her hands on her hips, shoulders raised protectively.

"Like what? Like I think you're incredible? Amazing? Sexy? Because I do."

Her skin had goose bumps, her nipples taut.

Since it was hotter than hell outside, he knew she wasn't cold.

"Like I'm a cell on a microscope slide."

He had to laugh at that. "Never once has looking at a cell from any organism given me a hard-on. I'm staring at you because I think you're gorgeous."

"Since when?" Her hand was reaching for her discarded shirt.

Lucas stopped her by grabbing her arm. He'd cry if she covered up those breasts after only sixty seconds. "Remember that summer you went away to camp to be a counselor?"

She nodded, hand still poised to grab her top. He knew she would if he let go of her wrist. "I was eighteen."

"When you came home, tanned and confident, laughing and excited, I watched you. And I realized that you were beautiful. You've only grown more so every year since then."

"Lucas . . ." she said, and it sounded like a warning, but her green eyes had gone soft.

He knew what her warning was. He knew now there was no time to take it slow, to hesitate, to savor Ashley. Not this time. She wasn't sure of him, her feelings, what they were doing, yet she wanted him. Lucas was sure that Ashley cared about him, maybe even loved him, given how she had treated him over the years. But she wasn't in love with him.

That was okay, because he planned to make love to her until she did fall in love with him. Or at the very least until she saw that they had something really solid to build a relationship on.

If she got cold feet, it would be over before they could even start.

So he had to take her so far into pleasure, she'd forget to think.

Instead of answering, he kissed her. Hard. With tongue.

She gasped.

He took the wrist he was holding and draped her arm around his back. He pulled them together. Then bent down and took her nipple into his mouth. She tasted warm and sensual, her nails digging into his back. Lucas sucked, and he licked, and he sucked, until she was whimpering and breathing hard. Until he grew rougher and rougher, nipping at her with his teeth, flicking along her breast with his tongue until he reached for the other one.

The room was quiet except for their heavy breathing and an occasional random moan from Ashley that spiked his temperature and sent him sweating. She tasted so damn good, so sweet and eager and he was so completely sure that he wanted to spend the rest of his life with her. When he cupped her ass, a tight firm cheek in each of his hands, Ashley swore.

"Shit, this feels good," she murmured.

"You're telling me." Lucas pulled his mouth back from her breasts as he slipped his hands under her skirt. Her panties were silky, tight across her backside, and low on her hips.

He wandered around, his thumbs landing on her soft mound. "It's very hot under here."

"I'm sure there's a purely biological reason for that," she said, her head tilted back. "Like that the proximity between my thighs raises the temperature."

"Or because, biologically speaking, your body wants to be fucked."

"Lucas!" She stared down at him, her mouth open as he dropped down onto one knee.

"What?" He pulled her skirt down, watched it puddle around her ankles, exposing her pink panties. Of course they were pink. Ashley was a pink kind of girl. "All the signs of arousal are here. Heavy breathing, tense muscles, heated flesh."

Ignoring her fingers pressing down hard on his shoulders, he skimmed his thumbs under her panty line, sinking one into her slickness. "Wet. Definitely aroused."

"So this is all about biology?" Her voice had gotten sharp. "My body is reacting to a stimulus? How flattering. I suppose that's what has happened to you too, then. Your body is reacting to the arousing image of all these sexual products and their functions."

He liked her outrage. It meant she cared. Lucas peeled down her panties. "No. Not at all. My body is reacting to seeing you naked. My body is reacting to the fact that my fantasy is finally coming to life. My body is reacting to the fact that I love you."

Ashley gasped. He so did not just say that. "What? You don't mean that!"

And oh, God, would he just stop stroking her like that,

right across her clitoris with the pad of his finger. She couldn't think, couldn't concentrate on anything but how she ached deep inside. About how good this felt. If she wasn't clinging to his shoulders, she swore she would have fallen over in a heap of quivering muscles.

But he couldn't love her. He couldn't.

"I do mean it."

Lucas was on his knees and Ashley realized that he was leaning forward, his mouth opening, heading right toward her like he was going to . . .

"You're not going to . . ."

His lips pressed against her curls, right over her clitoris. Bull's-eye. She jerked in surprise, in desire.

"Lucas, don't." Ashley wasn't a prude, not by any stretch of the imagination, given that she sold dildos to her friends, but she was standing up in her living room. She was naked, except for her panties still hooked around her thighs. Lucas was on his knees in front of her, and it was so damn sexy, yet so unnerving. Intimate.

"You're not, you can't, you won't," she babbled.

His tongue stroked her.

Oh, yes he was, could, would.

One of his hands was on her backside, holding her in place, the other spreading her apart for his mouth, and Ashley saw stars. Twisting his hair around her fingers, she held on for dear life as he moved over her again and again, his tongue incredibly talented. He dipped, he twirled, he slid deep inside her until her legs were shaking and her heart was racing.

She murmured, "Oh shit, oh shit, oh shit," as the tight burning need rose higher and higher. When she tried to ease away from him, afraid she'd shatter too soon, he just followed her, stalking her, never letting up for a second.

Desperate to get away, she almost fell off her stilettos. It felt so damn good, so hot, so wet, so perfect and she couldn't stop if he didn't stop.

The light from her teardrop crystal chandelier fell on Lucas's head, drawing out the caramel highlights in his hair. The hair that she was just about ripping out at the roots.

He pulled back far enough to murmur, "Come for me, Ashley. Please."

Like as if she were doing him some kind of favor. She would have laughed, except he buried his mouth in her and sucked her clitoris.

Her head snapped back, a low groan ripping out of her, as she exploded, spasms of pleasure rocking through her body. It was short, volcanic in intensity, and left her stunned. She shuddered, she shivered, she whimpered.

"Lucas, oh my God," she managed as she tried to re-member to breathe, her body still pulsing from the cata-clysmic orgasm.

Her legs wobbled when he let go of her. Somewhere in the back of her mind she realized he was ripping off his jeans, his briefs, tearing open a condom. But it didn't really register what that meant until he wrapped her leg around his thigh and slid into her, hard and possessive, sinking in like he owned the place.

Ashley came again. Immediately. And was so damn shocked that she did fall off her shoes, landing on the flat side of the sandals. Which only sent him deeper inside her as they both moaned.

Her inner muscles convulsed, her whole body tingled, as he pulled back and thrust up into her again. Going on her tiptoes, she kicked her slip-on shoes out of the way and held onto his chest, her forehead resting against his shoulder. She could smell his skin, a musky sensual scent, intermixed with the sweetness of her own desire rising between them.

He was moving in her, hard, steady strokes, and Ashley nipped his skin, wanting to taste him, wanting to feel and experience all of this moment. Everything felt hot, over-bright, sharply in focus. She was dizzy, out of control, hold-ing onto Lucas, thinking that this was something more, something deeper, than what she'd ever had with any other man.

Maybe it was because they knew each other so well. Because they cared.

Whatever it was, when Lucas groaned with ecstasy in her ear, he touched a spot in her heart that she hadn't even known existed. "Ash."

Then while she was overwhelmed, in awe, he came inside her with one last fast thrust. Squeezing her muscles around him to further his pleasure, Ashley watched his face, watched his eyes roll back, watched his jaw twitch, studied the dewy perspiration on his upper lip with a kind of feminine triumph.

She had done that.

He wanted her. Desired her. Lost his control in her.

And that made her feel very, very sexy.

"Whoa," he said, after he had stopped pulsing in her.

Ashley gave a soft laugh. "Is that your scientific conclusion?"

"Yes. Based on the fact that this was incredible."

"Yeah, it was, wasn't it?" Ashley kissed his shoulder, then eased herself off of him, and stepped back with a grin.

She felt fabulous, her body still tingling and shivering with aftershocks. It was the rush of running a marathon and winning. Or more accurately, like scoring big at a Nieman-Marcus sidewalk sale. Sexy shoes for five bucks.

The floor was sticky beneath her feet from humidity, and she stepped back into her stilettos, lifting herself up two inches. The room was hot, suffocating, and her hair was damp from sweat. Turning, she headed on wobbly legs toward the fan she had standing behind her dining room table.

"Where are you going?"

She glanced back at Lucas, who was watching her, one hand unrolling the condom, neither his erection nor his expression looking like he was finished for the night.

Good.

"Just turning on the fan. It's hot in here."

With a flip of the switch, it started up, blowing cool air across her heated body, sending delightful little shivers through her. It caressed her hot inner thighs, her hardened nipples, her tight belly, and she lifted the heavy hair up off her neck to dry the dampened curls.

"This feels good, Lucas. Come here."

The air dancing across her was turning her on, and she was hoping for round two.

"Coming."

Perfect.

Seven

Lucas wondered if Ashley had any idea what she looked like bent over that fan completely naked, wearing high heels.

Given the tone of her voice, he suspected she did. Which meant she wouldn't be shocked when he came up behind her and slid his cock back into her.

Because once wasn't enough for him. He didn't think a lifetime would be enough, but he was hoping to settle for that.

It was stifling in her apartment, a side effect of being on the second floor of a ninety-year-old house with the original windows. Her air-conditioning was twenty years old and mediocre, and the sun had pounded heavily all day. It was probably still seventy-five degrees outside and eighty in the house, even though it was eleven at night.

So there was definitely a need to stay naked. And Ashley looked so good doing it. She was bent just a little, enticingly, her back arching, the bumps of her spine curving gracefully. Her ass was high and firm, her waist dipping in so it created an hourglass shape. Those blond curls of hers blew behind her as she dug her fingers in the crown of her hair, her head tilted.

Lucas walked toward her, sweating from want more than from the heat. There was just something so unbelievably sexy about the lines of her body. He dropped down on his haunches and caressed her ankle.

Ashley jerked. "What are you doing down there?"

"Making my way up." The cool air from the fan came between her spread legs and hit him in the chest. Lucas licked the back of Ashley's calf, tracing the curve of the muscle to the back of her knee.

She sighed, the sound almost lost over the hum of the fan. He kissed the soft skin behind her knee, let his fingers follow along behind his mouth as he edged higher and higher, inch by luscious inch. Lucas let his eyes drift half closed, let himself hold onto her other leg and nudge his nose up to the underside of her ass.

"Lucas . . ." she said in that plaintive way she had of drawing out his name. She had always strung his name out, sometimes in humor, sometimes in annoyance, sometimes in affection, but he liked this way the best, the way she sounded so aroused, so shocked at her own reaction, so sure they were being naughty and yet liking it.

"Hmmm?" He got his head between her legs, urging her legs farther apart. "Hold onto the fan, baby."

She did, even as she was saying, "This is crazy, what are you doing?"

It took a little maneuvering, but he was able to twist and reach her soft inner folds. He spread her, blew on her swollen, slick, secret spot. "Cooling you off."

Her voice was strangled. "That's having the opposite effect."

Allowing one quick lick first, he retreated. "Sorry." But he had ascertained she was still moist, ready for him. Important information since he was about to stand up and enter her.

"No problem." Her breasts heaved and her eyes were clamped shut.

Lucas moved out from between her legs, enjoying the cry of disappointment she gave.

"That was cruel," she remarked. "What am I holding on to the fan for if you're leaving?"

"Because I'm planning on doing this." He aligned himself behind her, held her waist, and urged, "Bend over a little more."

"Why?" But she did it anyway, and he figured she had to know what it was he wanted.

Then he was nudging deep inside her, groaning as her vaginal muscles clamped around him and squeezed. "Is this cruel?"

Ashley clutched the fan and decided these shoes needed to be flung out the window. Lucas kept catching her off guard, and she was going to sprain an ankle with one false move. Since he had her straining and squirming and wiggling, it wouldn't be hard to take a tumble off the heels.

"If you start moving, I'll forgive you." For anything. Ever. For the rest of their lives. He seemed to know instinctively how to please her. And was doing it in spades.

"That can be arranged."

He was thick inside her, full, and when he moved, her tender swollen body ached with pleasure. "Lucas? Would it be rude if I came, like, right away?"

It was almost embarrassing how quick he could bring her to the point. She had never thought she was quite this easy. She was never really difficult, exactly, but usually she required more than three strokes.

Not now.

"No. That's what I want. I want you so turned on you can't help yourself."

"I think I can wait a second." Ashley licked her lips, which were rapidly drying from the fan blowing on her. There was something extra sexy about the cool air rushing over her hot body, teasing her nipples tight, while Lucas pounded into her.

"Don't wait too long. I'm about done."

"Oh!" Well. That changed everything. Ashley rested her head on her forearm and just felt. Just let her body absorb the thrusts, enjoy the brush of his testicles against her backside, and relax into the rhythm.

When he paused, then came in a silent orgasm, straining and digging his fingers into her waist, Ashley went right after him.

Only she didn't try to keep it quiet. She let out a yell to rival an Olympic shot putter. It encompassed all her excitement, pleasure, satisfaction, and a myriad of other emotions that she wasn't ready to deal with just yet.

Lucas's head dropped onto her back, his breath ragged as he stopped moving inside her. "Holy shit."

Her thoughts exactly. Ashley peeled her fingers back from the fan, not surprised to see deep grooves in them from the slats she'd been pressing against. "I'm going to fall down. My legs don't work anymore."

Lucas pulled out of her. "Couch. That's what we need." He took her hand and they stumbled the two feet to the sofa.

Ashley collapsed on him, letting her shoes drop off. Her breasts pressed into his chest and her thigh settled between his. With a sigh, she lay her head down on his shoulder, thinking it was much to heavy to keep upright any longer. "Well, this was unexpected. Incredible, but unexpected."

She meant the whole twist in their relationship, not just the second sex session so fast after the first, though that was pretty amazing too.

Lucas idly stroked her back, his mouth rubbing back and forth over the top of her hair.

"You could sell me anything right now, Ashley. I mean *anything*. That's how good I feel."

She laughed. Playing with his fawn-colored chest hairs, she let herself think about what Lucas had said. He had said he loved her.

What did that mean? She loved him too. Like a brother . . . well, okay, not exactly like a brother. But like a friend.

Only that wasn't right either, not when she was intertwined with his naked body. Not when it was very possible that she wanted to repeat this night. But there were so many complications, including her younger brother.

"What about Jason?" she said, thinking out loud, curious if Lucas had given any thought to what his best friend would think about what they were doing.

"What about him?" Lucas cupped her butt, squeezed a little.

"I don't think he'll like us doing this." Ashley had palpitations just thinking about her brother's reaction. He would be horrified. Furious with her. Of course, it was a little late to be worried about that since she was naked and Lucas had had her over an electric fan.

"I'm not sure it's really any of Jason's business. But why do you think he'll be upset?"

Distracted by the sight of his lips moving, so close to her, she ran her finger across the cherry redness of his lower lip.

He added, "You worried he won't think I'm good enough for his sister?"

That got her attention. What a joke. Ashley let her hand drop. "No, I think Jason thinks I'm not good enough for you! His best friend, fellow chemist, being defiled by his shopaholic, blond, brainless sister? I think he knows you can do better."

She hadn't meant to sound so whiny. But it was true. Jason had gotten the brains, and she had gotten the beauty. Her parents had told her that over and over, every time she brought home a "D" in Math on a report card or struggled through reading *Moby Dick*. She was destined to be in service, they'd said, since she was so good at smiling, being cheerful, making people happy. And what she resented was that they made that sound like it was less worthy than working in a laboratory. It wasn't, and at twenty-eight she knew that.

She hadn't at twenty-two, and getting a job at a computer design firm had been an act of defiance in some ways. Unfortunately the triumph was short-lived since she'd worked there five years and was still an entry-level employee.

Lucas frowned at her, his hand going still. "You're kidding me. Is that how you think Jason sees you? Is that how you think *I* see you?"

"Well . . ." Ashley didn't want to discuss this. She didn't know why she had sounded so needy. She didn't know why it mattered in the least what her parents or anyone else thought of her abilities. She knew who she was and she liked herself.

But the harsh truth was she was not the kind of woman Lucas Manning would want long term, no matter what his hormones thought. She would bore him senseless in under three weeks.

"Jason doesn't think you're brainless. And neither do I. In case you hadn't noticed, I think you're amazing. I think you're the most exciting, fun, beautiful, interesting woman I've ever known. I've known you for almost twenty years and I've always respected and admired you for who you are."

She winced. She hadn't meant to force him into extolling her virtues. "Thank you. I've always felt the same about you." But that didn't change the fact that they were intellectually incompatible.

Chances were good he would bore her too.

Only she knew that was a lie the minute the thought popped into her head. She had always liked Lucas, enjoyed his curiosity, his humility, so different from her brother, who bragged incessantly.

"I meant what I said before." Lucas turned on his side so he was facing her, chocolate eyes searching over her. "I love you."

His voice was so tender, so determined, that Ashley felt her resolve wavering. He sounded so damn sincere, and she felt that it would be so, so easy to just relax into her own feelings. It would only be a matter of a second and she could fall straight into love with Lucas.

It couldn't be that easy.

"We're complete opposites," she whispered. "You're responsible, I'm flighty. You have a master's degree and a title with a whole bunch of words I can't even pronounce, and I only graduated from college by a prayer."

Lucas didn't look concerned. He kissed her softly. "You have common sense, I have none. I have trouble remembering left from right and to turn the oven off when I'm done cooking. Don't you see, Ash? We balance each other."

She chewed her lip, wondering, worrying. It wasn't like her to get this worked up—usually she dove into relationships and thought later. Which was probably why they had all ended disastrously. And this was Lucas. Help her, she did love him, and she didn't want to hurt him, to mess this up.

"I know I'm annoying, Ash, I know I ask too many questions and I think too much instead of just doing things. But that's who I am, and I can't change that."

That got her attention. Ashley touched his cheek, horrified that he would think that about himself. "Oh, Lucas, don't say that. You're not annoying at all. I like that about you, I like that you stop and think everything through instead of just throwing yourself into it. I . . . I . . . "

Oh, dear God, she was going to say it. She'd never said this to any man, ever, and she was going to just blurt it out right now, naked on her couch, to Lucas, who was giving her one of those earnest looks she just absolutely adored.

"Yes?"

"I . . . I love you, Lucas. I do."

His brow wrinkled as he frowned. "You do?"

She nodded. "Yes." She did, she really, really did.

And she was scared shitless.

Eight

Lucas studied Ashley's face. She loved him. She. Loved. Him.

He hadn't seen that one coming.

He had hoped that someday, maybe, after much persuasive sex, she could be convinced that they could work out something permanent, and he knew that she cared about him . . . but in love with him?

That was beyond his greatest expectations.

"Like you love me like a friend, a brother, someone you've known your whole life?" He sought clarity of her statement.

"No, silly." She kissed him, moving her mouth over his softly.

Ashley tasted sweet, warm, and he liked the way she was sliding up against him, hand on his cheek, her touches tender and seeking. She pulled back and smiled.

"I love you like a woman loves a man. I love you in a way that is almost overwhelming, because it's so unexpected."

He kissed her fingertips resting on his lips, happiness crashing over him.

"But it's so strong, it seems to me that maybe somehow it's always been there, I just didn't know it."

Lucas couldn't say the same. "I always knew I loved you."

"Really?" She smiled, sighed, snuggled into his arms. "Why didn't you say something?"

He nearly laughed. "For all the reasons you just outlined. I didn't think you'd be interested in your little brother's geeky friend. Not when you were busy dating every high school football coach on the west side. I've never been into sports."

Ashley squeezed his bicep. "Though you have developed some sexy muscles. Why have you been hiding these from me?"

"I don't think I have been."

"Then I've clearly been an idiot because when I turned tonight and you were standing there with no shirt on, jeans, barefoot, I about had an orgasm just looking at you."

Now that was a sexy little image. And it was good information for future seductions.

"Now just to recap what we've established here, Ash. I love you, you love me, we're sexually compatible, and our personalities are the perfect complement to each other. Right?"

She nodded.

"So we can consider ourselves together. Permanently." He liked to know where he stood.

Her cheeks lost their color. "But Lucas, don't forget I'm older than you. When I'm forty, you'll only be thirty-six."

"But I'll be forty in my heart," he said, with a perfectly straight face, even though he was being sarcastic. He thought a less than four-year age difference between them meant absolutely nothing. Less than nothing. Negative relevance.

She smacked his back. "I'm serious. I'll be all old and haggard at eighty and you'll only be seventy-six."

"I don't think it matters at that point. We'll both have plastic parts and wrinkles." But just the thought of spending his whole life with Ashley made him grin. "Now drop the age thing, Ash. It doesn't mean a damn thing."

"But . . ."

He cut her off. "I have a tickle-whip, remember? And I'm not afraid to use it."

Her green eyes went wide. "What do you mean?" She licked her lips.

Hot damn. She was so sexy. He patted her ass. "I mean, if you don't stop borrowing trouble and looking for excuses, I'll have to use whatever means necessary to convince you we're perfect for each other."

Breath catching, eyes half closed, she rubbed against him in a way that had him groaning.

"Could you maybe do your convincing in my bedroom? This couch isn't really comfortable, Lucas."

"I can do that." He sat up, pulled her into his lap. "And maybe this time we'll actually make it to a supine position."

"What is that? It sounds kinky." She shivered with delight, the sound hitting his ears at the same time her hot wet center slid against his cock.

Lucas bit back a groan. "It just means lying down on your back, faceup. Which we won't get to if you don't stop doing that."

"Doing what?" she said, even as she lifted her hips and rocked on him again.

"Driving me crazy." Lucas set Ashley firmly away from him and stood up. He shook out his legs, every muscle sore. "Now where are all my purchases?" he said, to tease her. "Let's take them into the bedroom with us, and you can show me how they work."

Not that he didn't already have an idea what to do with them, but it might be fun to play dumb. Let her give him step-by-step instructions.

Ashley's eyebrows rose. "*All* of your purchases? At one time?"

Lucas thought through what he'd bought. Blindfold,

handcuffs . . . *sure, why not?* Peachy eating powder stuff, *definitely he wanted that.* Tickle-whip . . . *yes, yes, and fuck, yes.*

She grinned. "Even the cock ring?"

Damn, he'd forgotten about that thing. "Sure," he said reluctantly. Maybe he could kick it under the bed and pretend it was lost. It wouldn't be that difficult to pop it either, he imagined. It was just soft plastic. "And the Ben-Wa balls."

Ashley's grin disappeared, though her breath caught. "We don't need any of that junk, Lucas. All we need is each other."

"True. Very true." He heartily agreed, except for one thing. He took her hand, started walking toward her bedroom, right past the tables of products. Spotting what he was looking for, he paused, turned to pull her into his arms.

"Ashley, I love you." He kissed the side of her jaw, kissed her bottom lip, kissed her nose, knowing there was nothing logical about his feelings for her, but for once in his life not needing the answers.

Ashley pressed her body to his, going up on her tiptoes to kiss him. "I love you too, Lucas."

He reached behind him on the table, his fingers closing around what he wanted. Flicking it open, he slapped one ring of the fur-lined handcuffs on her wrist and clicked it shut.

"What is that?" Ashley jerked back in shock, but he was already attaching the other end to his own wrist. "Lucas! You handcuffed us together!"

"That was the plan." He gave a jerk to test them. Ashley's arm flew toward him. The leopard print fur was soft and comfortable against his skin. "I'm going to leave these on until you agree that we're perfect for each other. That we'd be stupid not to go for it."

"Are you calling me stupid?" She flashed him a big

smile, showing all her straight, white teeth. They were away from the light and half of her face was in shadows.

Something in his gut told him now was the time. Go for it. Grab for everything he had ever wanted. "I'll think you are if you don't say yes."

"To what?" She put her hands on her hips, which meant his hand had to rest there too.

"To getting married."

"Married?" Her jaw dropped. "Married?"

Ashley slapped her hand over her mouth. Oh, God, he was serious. He was completely and totally serious. He was giving her that look—that intense, expectant look.

"But we just . . . but we just . . ." she babbled, not sure what to say. It would be absurdly impulsive to say yes. It would be irresponsible to just leap into something so incredibly important as marriage without thinking it through.

Too bad she wanted to say yes. She wanted to be with Lucas forever. She wanted to make him laugh, and she wanted to feel his hand steady on her back.

And Lucas was logical, to the very depths of his soul. If he thought this made sense, then surely it must.

It was time to trust her own instincts.

"Okay. Yes."

Now he was the one who looked floored. "Really?"

She laughed, joy rising up in her. "You're the one who said we're perfect for each other."

"We are." He wrapped his one arm tighter around her. "But I thought I would have to do some convincing."

Then he brushed her lips with his, and she wanted to cry at the tenderness of it.

"Damn, you've made me so happy." His kiss was full of passion and love, his tongue gliding across hers.

She sighed. "Oh, Lucas, me too."

"I love the way you say my name." Then he shook their hands linked together and grinned. "We can take the cuffs off if you want. Or leave them." He gave her a wicked wink.

Ashley nearly came on the spot, but she thought handcuffs were more than she could handle at this point. Her emotions, her body, were all on sensory overload. Any more stimuli and she might wind up in a puddle on the floor. "We can take them off."

"How do we get them off?" he asked.

She stared at him blankly. "I don't know."

"What do you mean you don't know?" Lucas pulled their hands up to eye-level and studied the cuffs. "What did the directions say?"

Feeling a little panicked, she said, "I told you, I didn't try all these products. In fact, I didn't try any of them. I just read my Pleasure Party consultant manual."

Lucas didn't look particularly worried. He just said, "Well, I guess we leave the cuffs on, then."

What if she had to go to the bathroom? Needed a shower? Who were they going to ask to get these things off? They were naked, damn it, they couldn't just flag down a neighbor. "That's it? That's all you're going to say? You don't have some complex method of melting these cuffs off of us?"

"No." He shrugged. "I'm not wearing any clothes and I'm handcuffed to the woman of my dreams with very soft, furry cuffs. I'm not about to complain."

"That's a very male attitude." But she could see his point. It had to be almost midnight. There was nothing they could do about the situation right this second, unless she wanted to dig through all her paperwork to try and find the handcuffs' directions.

It made more sense to look for them in the morning.

"I'm a male, what can I say?"

Ashley closed her free hand over his penis and cupped it. "Mmm, yes, you definitely are."

He groaned.

She stroked up and down, pleased at his immediate reaction. He had swelled into a nice, thick rod under her fingers.

"We're not going to make it to the bedroom, are we?" she asked.

"If we hurry, we still can." He gripped her elbow, forced her hand to stop moving over him. "Let's go. One, two, three . . . run."

Neither one of them took a single step.

"Let's just get *supine* on these tables," she said, trying to push him backward by leaning against him.

He planted his feet apart and didn't budge, though somehow mysteriously his fingers had wound up between her thighs, exploring and stroking and digging through her curls to her clitoris. "I don't think those tables can hold us. The one right behind us is a card table, Ash."

"Then we'll have to improvise." Ashley dropped to her knees in front of Lucas, keeping her left wrist up near his waist so she didn't pull him down.

He swore. "What are you doing?"

"Isn't it obvious? I'm improvising." She brushed her fingers over the soft hairs on his thigh and ran her lips over the satin smooth skin of his hard penis. "It's so hot, so silky."

Lucas grunted.

She licked along the side of his shaft, from the tip, past the ridge, down to the end, then back up again. Holding him in her hand, she rolled her tongue over the top, taking up the salty clear fluid hovering there.

His fingers buried in her hair, digging harder and harder into her scalp, encouraged her. Excited her.

Emboldened her.

She closed her mouth around him and took him deep inside. Breath rushed out her nose as she rolled her eyes back in ecstasy. He tasted so damn good. She pulled back, filled her mouth again.

Lucas gripped her head harder, making little low growling sounds in the back of his throat. Desire gripped her in a tight little knot right between her legs as she sucked faster, her lips sliding along the moisture she left behind, her movements losing finesse as she lost control.

"Oh, damn, Ashley." Lucas started moving his hips, meeting her halfway with urgent thrusts.

She closed her eyes, gripped his thigh, letting the taste and sound and scent of him wash over her. Everything was different. Her whole world had shifted today.

Instead of finding a lucrative side job, she had found something she hadn't even known she'd been looking for. Love. With a man who had been right under her nose her entire life.

It felt so right, so wonderful, so passionate to share her future with Lucas.

She let her hand that was cuffed go slack, dangling in the fur and held up by Lucas, so she could concentrate on stroking with her mouth, sucking in her cheeks, and enjoying his body. There was no hesitation on either of their parts, and everything with Lucas was erotic, sensual, safe, comfortable.

And when he exploded in her, she was very, very pleased.

Nine

Ashley woke up feeling extremely satisfied and sore. Lying on her back, a thin sheet pulled over her naked body, Ashley pried her eyes open.

And saw her brother standing in the door of her bedroom looking like he'd been smacked in the face with a two-by-four. His mouth moved, but no sound came out.

"Jason!" She darted a glance to her left, hoping somehow Lucas had miraculously separated himself from her and was in the shower. No such luck. He was still cuffed to her, sprawled out on his stomach, without a stitch on him. The sheet was shoved toward her in a messy heap, leaving him completely bare.

"Umm . . . sorry." Jason closed his eyes. "I didn't know you, uh, had someone here." Her brother's cheeks were bright red. "I was just looking for Lucas. We were supposed to go golfing this morning and he's not home. Lucas has never stood me up for anything. I was just wondering if you knew where he was."

Ashley clutched the sheet to her chest and gawked at her brother. Jason didn't even realize that was Lucas lying next to her. It was almost funny. "Why didn't you just knock?" she demanded, starting to enjoy her brother's discomfort.

He covered his face with one hand, rubbed vigorously. Jason was wearing a crisp red golf shirt and khaki pants, looking efficient and clipped and confident, like he always did. Except a mug of coffee was shaking just a little in his free hand. She knew that hot pink mug with the funky daisies on it. It had come from her kitchen.

"I used my key because I wanted to see if you had anything to eat, but I didn't want to disturb you if you weren't awake."

"This is what you get for stealing my food."

"Yeah, well, I've lost my appetite now."

She laughed. The shoe was on the other foot now. "I guess we're even then. Hope was at my Pleasure Party last night and trust me, I heard *way* more than I ever wanted to know about your sex life."

"Hope was here?" Interest crept into Jason's voice. "What did she buy?"

"I can't tell you. That would be violating my customer confidentiality."

"Oh, come on! She's my girlfriend. You're my sister."

Since Jason still had his eyes closed, Ashley leaned over the side of the bed, hoping there might be a stray T-shirt lying around. Unfortunately, she forgot she was connected to Lucas. She yanked his arm a foot before she realized it.

Lucas groaned. "Ash, you just ripped my shoulder out of the socket."

Ashley winced and fell back against her pillow. "Sorry."

Jason's hand fell off his face. "Lucas?" His eyes popped open. Then bugged out. "What the *hell* am I looking at?"

Lucas lifted his head and shot a bleary glance at Jason. "Oh, hey, Jason."

Ashley twitched the sheet over Lucas's butt and prayed a shark would swallow her whole. This was so embarrassing.

"Umm, well, Lucas and I . . ." *Had hot monkey sex.*

"Well, no shit!" Jason said in exasperation. "What I

want to know is why my best friend and my big sister are getting it on with each other?"

"That's a stupid question, man." Lucas yawned. "Give me ten minutes to shower and I'll meet you downstairs."

"Lucas, honey?" Ashley cleared her throat. "Aren't you forgetting something?" She lifted her hand up, and by default his.

"You *handcuffed* my sister?" Jason set his coffee down on her dresser, his face going from red to an alarming shade of plum purple. "That's it, I am so going to kick your ass."

"No!" Ashley squeaked, ready to fling herself over Lucas if need be.

But Lucas just snorted. "Relax, Jason, we were just goofing around. Can you go look through Ashley's Pleasure Party stuff and find the key? It's probably in the box the handcuffs came in."

"Oh my God. I'm going to be sick." Jason backed out of the room. "You're a dead man, Manning. Here you are, my best friend, and I trusted you to look after my sister for all these years, and this is how you repay me? I'm going to kick your ass the minute the cuffs come off."

"We're getting married," Ashley said.

Her words were smothered under a blanket of testosterone.

"You couldn't kick my ass with the cuffs still *on*." Lucas rolled onto his back and eyeballed her brother. "And I have looked out for Ashley. More than you have."

"What the fuck is that supposed to mean?" Jason's hands curled into fists.

Ashley rolled her eyes. This brotherly concern was touching and all, but they both seemed to be missing the point. "We're getting married."

No one heard her.

"It means that all these years Ashley's been thinking she's the family dumb blonde and you let her think that. You talk down to her and that's not cool."

Oh, that was throwing a big old glob of chicken fat on the fire.

"I don't think of Ashley as a dumb blonde. Do I, Ash?" Jason looked absolutely affronted.

Since he'd been telling blonde jokes just about since he'd started speaking at eight months old, she wasn't sure why he looked so startled. "Well, actually, Jason, you average about three blonde digs a week. You introduce me as your beautiful, but not very bright sister, and at one point suggested I would make a hell of a shampoo girl."

He frowned. "I said that?"

"Yeah." It was burned into her memory. Lucas's hand caressed her back, giving silent comfort.

"Well, that's because you're my sister, I care about you. It's my way of ribbing you, like a brother should. Like when I give you a hard time about shopping. It's because I'm really proud of you. I mean, you're gorgeous, and you always look like you stepped out of a magazine. What guy wouldn't want a sister so classy? But I couldn't let you get an ego about it."

"No chance of that." But her hurt feelings started to ebb, as she realized something for the first time. Jason looked confused, the poor guy. Maybe he wasn't so smart after all. At least she understood people, which was obviously more than she could say for him.

"Look, I'm sorry if any of that stuff bothered you. I didn't mean to hurt you, Ash."

She could see that, and it was a huge relief. It wasn't Jason's fault they had never talked about this before. He couldn't have known it bothered her if she never said anything. And she had always loved her brother, known he cared about her. "I believe you, Jason. It's okay."

"You were always so popular, so good with people. I never had any of that. My only friends were Lucas and the guys in the chess club." Jason grinned. "They all thought you were so hot. When we were in eighth grade and you were a junior, they all paid me five bucks to walk through your bedroom and touch your cheerleading uniform."

All the fuzzy warm feelings she'd been having evaporated. "What? Jason Andrews! That's horrible." She threw her pillow at him and turned to glare at Lucas.

He held up his hand. "Don't look at me. I didn't pay five bucks to touch your pom-poms."

"Nah. I let him do it for free."

"You didn't!" Ashley gaped at Lucas, who looked painfully guilty.

"I didn't actually *touch* anything, I just sort of walked around your room." He scratched the whiskers sprinkling across his chin and shot Jason a dirty look.

"Oh, my God. You're both twisted." Ashley shifted on the bed, a little stunned that she had been the object of Lucas's teenage fantasies. "Now, Jason, can you get out so I can get dressed? And please go find the key."

"Sure." Jason snorted and started to turn.

"We're getting married, Jason," Lucas said, his words arresting her brother.

How come no one heard her when she had said that?

Jason turned back around, looking horror-stricken. "Very funny." He gave a forced chuckle. "You had me for a second there."

"I'm serious."

They locked eyes. Stared each other down. Jason's gaze shifted to her. "Is he shitting me?"

She shook her head. "No. I'm in love with Lucas." Geez, it was so exciting to say that out loud. It felt so right, so real. Like it had always been there, and she hadn't known it. Ashley's cheeks grew hot, even as Lucas squeezed her hand, kissed the top of her head.

"Oh. Oh. Well." Jason shuffled his feet. "Marriage, huh?" Then his face split into a grin. He crossed the room and punched Lucas in the arm, gave him a half hug, with thumps on the back. "Dude, we'll be brothers for real! That's so cool."

Put out at being neglected, she said, "Hello . . . big sister here, planning a wedding, going to wear white . . . where's my hug?"

Jason spared her a glance. "You're naked, Ash. I'm not hugging you. And you might want to rethink the wearing white thing. Not very believable since you handcuffed yourself to a guy."

Idiot. "Lucas is naked too," she pointed out.

Jason jumped back. She grinned in satisfaction.

Lucas laughed at the mischievous look on Ashley's face. She knew how to rile up her brother.

For that matter, she knew how to rile him up too, but in a different way altogether.

Knowing he was grinning like the village idiot, Lucas wrapped his arm around Ashley and pulled her to him for a kiss. Her mouth was swollen, soft, her morning taste earthy, her curls tousled, her cheek still bearing the imprint of her pillow.

He was going to get to wake to this sight every single day for the rest of his life. He couldn't imagine how he'd gotten so damn lucky.

"If I find the handcuff key will you still go golfing with me?" Jason called from the living room, his lingering presence extremely unwanted.

Lucas did have to admit it was cool to think that Jason was going to be family now, officially. And he wouldn't have to worry about liking his wife's relatives. He already knew them all, and thought of Mr. and Mrs. Andrews like a second set of parents.

He would prefer to stay and roll around in some peach powder with Ash, but he had made the plans with Jason first.

"Do you mind, Ash? We've had this tee time booked for a couple of weeks." Lucas didn't want to leave her, but she might want to actually get some real sleep. "I can come over later and help you pack up the dildos." He owed those dildos a huge debt. They had brought him to Ashley's apartment last night. The least he could do was pack them in bubble wrap.

"Go golfing. I feel so good, this calls for shopping. But first, I have to visit my mom and my friends and every person I've ever met in my life and brag that I'm marrying the sexiest, smartest, most amazing man in existence."

"Do I know him?" Lucas joked, kissing each of her eyelids.

"Lucas," she sighed. "I do love you."

"I feel exactly the same. I've loved you for forever." It was perfectly logical, the smartest thing he'd ever done—falling in love with Ashley.

"Hey, guys? I'm not finding any key," Jason called from the other room. "But I did find some things I want to buy. This sex sling has potential."

Ashley rolled her eyes, groaned. But she was laughing. "He's never going to leave, is he?"

Lucas grinned, lay back down on the bed, and pulled Ashley over top of him. "I don't think so."

"We should get dressed."

"In a minute." Or a year.

"Ashley, what's a Mr. Right Now?" Jason yelled.

With an exasperated groan, she turned and called to him over her shoulder, "Why?"

"Well, these papers all sort of fell on the floor, and I was picking them up and I accidentally saw Hope's order form. She bought a Mr. Right Now."

"Accidentally?" Ashley snorted.

Lucas figured Jason's peek was as much of an accident as him making love to Ashley over a fan. It was more taking advantage of an opportunity than an accident, and he didn't think he could fault Jason for that.

"So what is it?" Jason asked again.

Ashley glanced down at Lucas and gave him a wink. Then she said, "There's a brochure sitting on the table. Read the description."

Lucas grew somewhat curious, his mind starting to spin possibilities for what could be given a title like that. "What is it?" he murmured, suddenly very aware of the press of Ashley's firm breasts against his chest. Her warm, moist sex resting over his cock.

"Use your imagination."

They were under the sheet, sticky and close, and Lucas had a very active imagination.

Jason's head popped into the bedroom. "Here's the handcuffs key." He threw a key dangling from a leopard striped plastic key chain in their direction. "We'll go golfing another time, Lucas. I just remembered something I need to tell Hope."

Lucas just bet he did. Then Jason was gone, and Ashley grinned at him.

"Worked like a charm," she whispered.

"Smart girl."

Ashley wiggled appealingly over top of him, and winked. "Now let's have our own Pleasure Party."

Hell, yeah. He could do that. Lucas planted his hand on her backside. "Sell it to me, Ash. I'll buy anything."

THE CUPID
CURSE

Jen Nicholas

Prologue

December 15, 2003
Tasha's Apartment

"I've decided what I want for my birthday." Valentine Lewis scooped up another bite of blueberry cheesecake and almost shivered at the delightful taste.

Tasha glanced up from her strawberry low-fat frozen yogurt and eyed her sister with apparent wariness. "Uh-huh. And that would be what?"

Val smiled and wiggled her eyebrows up and down a few times. "A man."

Tasha choked and made a grab for her water glass. "A man? Valentine Lewis wants a man? Are you insane?"

Val laughed and went back to the cheesecake. Using her fork like a conductor's baton, she proceeded to make her point with her sister. "Look. My birthday is on St. Valentine's Day, right? And my name is, of course, Valen-tine. Granted, the name makes me sick. But not much I can do about it now, is there? Anyway," she continued, scooping up a huge glob of cake and stuffing it in her mouth, "it's been, what, two years since I've had sex? I think it's a damn fine birthday present."

Tasha had stopped choking, but was now staring at her sister as if an alien had invaded her body. "I've got all that. But Val, you hate men."

Val snorted. "I don't hate men. I just happen to think that they're stupid, Neanderthal creatures who only think with one thing, and it's not their brains."

"Exactly."

"And," Val continued, watching Tasha roll her eyes, "most men are, in fact, a whole hell of a lot like Ziploc bags."

"Oh, dear God, Val, another analogy between men and totally obscure, inanimate objects?"

Val grinned at her sister. "Yep, but this one is the most apropos yet. Men, like Ziploc bags, are not only see-through, but they each claim to have a tight seal, and then willingly open wide for anyone who fiddles with their zipper."

"You"—Tasha said, waving her spoon at her lovable yet totally crazy sister—"are a certifiable man-hater." She stared closely at Val, wondering if she'd taken some type of medication recently and forgotten to tell her. "So why in God's name would you want a man for your birthday?"

Val sighed the sigh of infinite patience. "Because it's time. Tasha, I'm twenty-seven years old, will be twenty-eight in just a few more weeks. I haven't had sex in two years. Because, believe it or not, I do want a home and a family some day. And if I don't get my butt in gear, and soon, I'm going to die a dried-up old maid with only myself and my younger sister for company. Not that you're bad company, mind you," she added with a smile.

"Val, I understand that. I really do. But darn it, Val, for the last time, *you hate men!* And if that wasn't enough, just how do you expect to conjure up a man in time for your birthday? Not to mention that it's the most romantic time of the year." Tasha grabbed her sister's hand, trying to make her understand the craziness of the situation. "Internet dating? Singles bars? What!"

Val smiled her sassy smile and squeezed her sister's hand. "Relax, Tasha, I've got it all figured out. I'm simply going to ask Cupid."

One

January 4, 2004
Andersonville Public Library

In about three more seconds, Valentine Lewis was going to break the cardinal rule invisibly posted in all libraries—she was going to start screaming her head off.

She'd been doing research for six hours. *Six hours.* She'd used the library's massive computer system, she'd looked up every book listed in the online catalog, and she'd even, God help her, ruined her eyesight for life by flipping through thousands of screens of microfiche films.

All of that, and she'd still come up empty-handed. The library associates, she had to admit, had done their part to assist her. Everything she'd asked for, they'd brought to her with smiles. Granted, after the first four hours the smiles had started to become strained and their lips had started to take on the harshness of a Vulcan glare at the edges, but Val had to give them credit, they were still smiles.

Two more books. Two flimsy old books were now all that she had left before her to gain some vast well of knowledge. Actually, at this point, she'd settle for a small sesame seed–sized bit of knowledge. The books left for her perusal, however, didn't look very promising as both looked worse for wear. Cracked spines, torn edges, paper that was beginning to flake in spots was now her last hope. One was about a hundred pages long and written in such small print that she was afraid that she'd go blind trying to decipher it.

The other one looked downright pathetic, in both style and length. It was only about twenty pages in length, and the writing wasn't even typeset printing. It was handwritten in a delicate, almost feminine cursive style that, although pleasing to the eye, looked to be about the length of her grandmother's strawberry shortcake recipe.

Val sighed and gave up on the task of flipping through the tome of munchkin-sized typeset. She dragged the forlorn-looking recipe book toward her, sparing a tired and slightly blurred glance at the title. *The Cannons of Cupid.* To Val, it sounded like Cupid and his cohorts had taken over a brigadier ship.

Since it wasn't very long, she decided that this book, her last hope to gain insight into the life and times of Cupid, wasn't one to skim through. She'd read it from start to finish, and there had better be, by God, some scrap of hope that she could grab on to.

Val stretched her long legs out, resting them on top of the chair across the table from her. She pushed her long hair away from her face and rubbed a tired, ink-stained hand across her eyes. She took a deep breath, gave up a little prayer, and began reading.

She read the first seventeen or so pages in about five minutes, dreading the minute she would come to the last page. Another dead end. Another lost cause. Another . . .

". . . so as the Cannons dictate, Cupid is incapable of turning down any plea that is deigned to be genuine and heartfelt. All requests for assistance must thus be realized, and Cupid is required, by the dictates of law, to render his full aid and commitment to said pleas."

Val's half-yelp of delight echoed throughout the library, and as the stunned patrons and once-helpful assistants turned to her with a look of horror, she couldn't help but grin in what she hoped was an appeasing way. She might have broken one rule, but she'd finally found another that was destined to change her life.

January 6, 2004
Val's Apartment

Today was the day. Val sat at her desk, an open and blank journal of white paper before her. She'd read through the book again, that font of information, *The Cannons of Cupid*. Since she'd checked it out from the library two days ago, she'd read and reread it at least a dozen times.

Although there didn't seem to be anything else of importance except for that one passage, Val didn't despair. It could be that she just didn't understand the rest of the rules. This one, though, about making a heartfelt and genuine plea for assistance, she understood loud and clear.

And now it was time. Val had decided that she'd gleaned all that she could from those few sentences. She'd spent another day debating over whether her plea had to be spoken aloud, or if it could be written down. Everyone said that Val had a way with words. The problem was, those words had to be put down on paper. Spoken aloud, they just didn't seem to have the same effect.

After much inner debate and rereading, she decided that if her plea was good enough, if it was *heartfelt* and *genuine* enough, Cupid wouldn't give a rat's ass whether it was spoken aloud or written down on low-grade paper.

So now it was time to write her plea.

"Heartfelt and genuine. Heartfelt and genuine." She whispered the words fervently under her breath.

It was her new mantra. The previous one had been "one

day at a time," and before that it was "Mr. Allen is not a bloodsucking, perverted alien from Hell." Mr. Allen was her boss, and she'd decided he wasn't, after all, either from Hell or a bloodsucker, but a year later, he was still a pervert.

Her mind was wandering. She was nervous. This plea, this call for help, was her last resort. Tasha had thought she'd gone crazy when, a week before Christmas, Val had stated her intention to seek Cupid's help in finding a man.

Val twirled her pen restlessly between her fingers. Maybe she was a tad crazy. No one could grow up with the name Valentine and not be a little insane. Especially a grown woman of twenty-seven whose birthday just so happened to conveniently fall on St. Valentine's Day.

Tasha had wondered aloud if her desire to suddenly find a soul mate had come from the dual traumas of her name and date of birth. And maybe it had. But that wasn't all of it. Oh, Val admitted that Tasha wasn't all wrong in saying that she hated men. For years, millennia it seemed, she'd avoided men like the plague. From her past experiences with them, she had believed for a very long time that they were all immature idiots only interested in one thing—and it wasn't world peace.

But lately Val had been wondering if she'd been thinking about it all wrong. Granted, there would always be men who thought with a body part other than their brain. There would always be men in their forties who wanted to look and act as if they still lived somewhere back in the seventies. And there would, Lord help us all, always be men who assumed that women were complete morons, complete nerds, or complete baby-making machines.

But always didn't mean all. Just as there were women who made a living chasing men and then wringing them for all they were worth, they were the exception, not the rule. The same had to be true for men. For every bad one, Val hoped on all that was holy that there would be a good one.

She just hadn't found him yet.

As she doodled a heart with a matching arrow on her first blank sheet of paper, she again wished silently that her plan would work. Cupid, after all, was the epitome of love and romance. Throughout the ages people had relied on him to provide them with a suitable person to love. And when she'd done her research, she'd learned that men and women thousands of years ago had done the same, some even worshipping him as a god.

Although Val doubted that Cupid and God were one and the same, she did hope that he had some of the same abilities. Maybe they called each other on special occasions, or had powwows once a year.

But she'd put her chore off long enough. It was time. *Heartfelt* and *genuine*. That's all she had to do, all she had to be. Tell the truth, the whole truth, and nothing but the truth. So help her Cupid.

To Whom It May Concern:

First off, I have to admit that I'm not sure of the proper protocol on how to go about this, so I apologize in advance for any errors that I'm bound to make. The fact is, I'm desperate, and if it weren't for that fact, I probably wouldn't even be writing this letter. Hopefully, my honesty will lend me some credibility.

I suppose I should start with the basics. You may already know all of these things, but since I'm not one hundred percent sure of your abilities (I know they're great, I just don't know how far-reaching they are) I figure that to plead my case you'll need all of the details I can give you.

My name is Valentine Lewis. I was born on February 14, 1975, at Andersonville County Hospital in Illinois. I have wonderful parents, Don and Jaqueline, and the best younger sister, Tasha. I had a great child-

hood that I remember with fondness, and as far as I can tell, I have yet to suffer any great abuse or life-altering altercations.

That said, my life sucks.

Okay, okay, maybe that's a little harsh. It doesn't suck exactly, it just seems to be going downhill at an incredibly swift pace. I love my family, I love the great friends that I have, and except for my perverted boss, I even love my job. (By the way, I'm an accountant, and even though it sounds boring, I like it.) So maybe I shouldn't even be complaining. But the fact is I'm lonely.

It's not just the sex. Well, part of it, I'm sure, is the sex. Or in this case, the lack thereof. But even though I'd like to be able to remember what sex is, the loneliness is what's getting to me. I get up, I go to work, I come home, I eat, and I watch TV . . . alone. Always alone, and even though I thought that alone was what I wanted, it's starting to wear on my nerves. And my libido.

Am I even allowed to talk about libidos with you? See, I am so messed up, that never mind that I'm writing to Cupid, now I'm telling you about my pathetic sex life.

Anyway, back on track. I'm tired of being alone, and past experience has shown me that I'm no good at finding someone to change my status. As I'm sure you know, I have failed miserably at every past relationship that I've been in. I even admit that the majority of problems have been my fault.

I'm bossy. I'm picky about certain things. I'm stubborn and hardheaded and often speak before I thoroughly think things through. I'm a slob at home and a neat freak at work. I talk too much, sometimes quite loudly, and I don't have any qualms about laughing until my sides ache in public, or crying at a sad book, or burping when I've just eaten spicy food. In essence, I'm not exactly perfect girlfriend, lover, wife material.

That said, I also have my good points. I'm very outgoing, easy to talk to, and can keep a secret. I value my friendships and will do anything for those that I love. I'm a great cook, I actually like to do laundry, and I don't smoke, do drugs, or sleep around. (Moot point, here, isn't it?) I'm a hard worker, friendly and personable, and when I find a man to love, I will love him with my entire heart, body, mind, and soul.

Problem is, I can't find a man who will do the same in return. And that, Cupid, is why I'm asking for your help. You have a certain reputation for helping those who are romantically challenged. Love-handicapped, as it were. And if ever there was someone with a need, it would be me.

I don't even care to ask specifics in what I'd like. The old cliché is true . . . you can't judge a book by its cover. Size and shape, coloring and the size of the pectoral muscles don't matter. I just want a man who's kind and generous, who is sensitive when it's required but can offer me the strength that I need to complement myself. A man who's dedicated and loving, and although I'd like him to be sexual, if you could avoid dysfunctional or perverted, it would be greatly appreciated. I've had enough of those to last me several lifetimes.

I'm sure you know what I mean. A man that I can be proud to introduce to my family, and then can take home for some intimate entertainment. A strong character who isn't afraid to try new things, but who respects me when I say no.

I think that's about it. I have to admit that I have no idea whether this will work or not, but I've poured out my heart to you in the hopes that you can help. Any and all assistance will be greatly appreciated, and I thank you again for being the master of romance that you are.

Sincerely,
Valentine Lewis

January 7, 2004
Cupid Headquarters

"Cupid on a comet."

The words were spoken in a shocked voice of amazement, yet Gideon didn't even bother to look up from the book he was reading on the desk before him.

He managed to keep his attention on the written words through the long, low whistle that followed, and even through the "oh gosh" and "oh my" that followed the whistle. It wasn't until the man who shared an office with him stuck a sheaf of papers in front of his face that he tore his gaze away from what he was reading.

"I'm guessing you've gone blind, McCabe, since you obviously can't see that I'm busy."

McCabe's response was to prop his hip against Gideon's desk and slap the papers he'd been waving in his face against one thigh.

"You will never guess what this is."

Gideon spared a quick glance at the papers in McCabe's hand, then looked up with a scowl.

"My wild guess here is going to be paper."

"Come on, Gideon, don't be such a winger."

Gideon arched an eyebrow at his friend's choice of words, attempting to control his rising annoyance. McCabe knew how much he hated being called a winger. Winger . . . the Cupid term for a trainee. Winger . . . that slightly derogatory word that implied lower intelligence. Winger . . . just the sound of it made him want to unfurl one of said wings and smack McCabe upside the head with it.

"I'm not going to waste time reminding you for the umpteenth time how much I hate that word. So since we're in agreement that those are, indeed, papers, can you get on with whatever it is you want?"

"Fine. But you're still acting like a winger. Anyway," he continued, before Gideon could get off an appropriate response, "this, my good man, is your ticket to the big leagues."

"What are you talking about?"

McCabe shoved the papers at him, and Gideon reached out to grab them before he suffered a paper cut to the eye.

He looked down at the papers in his hand and then tossed them onto his desk. "Well, whoopee, McCabe, it's another RFA form. Just like the other two thousand RFA forms that you have sitting over there in your in-box."

"Gideon, sometimes you are such an idiot. I *know* it's an RFA form. I *know* it's a standard form, and that our office is inundated with them on a daily basis. But for goodness sake, would you please just *look* at the thing before you get all huffy with me?"

Gideon sighed and rubbed his hands briskly over his face. He'd been doing nothing but studying for the past hour and a half, cramming all of the information he could into his brain at one time. His Cupid Exams were coming up in just over a month, and he still had seventeen more books to study after this one. Seventeen. The thought alone had him sweating.

"Fine. Fine, fine, fine, I'll read it. If it will make you happy and shut you up, I'll read *this* Request For Assistance form just like I read the other five million we've done already this year."

He snatched up the papers from on top of his study book, pushed his chair back into the reclining position, and propped his long legs onto the top of his desk.

Then he sat up so hard and so fast that he unconsciously unfurled his wings, accidentally knocking McCabe upside the head after all.

Score one for the winger.

"Sorry," he mumbled, running his palm over the papers to smooth them out.

"No you're not," McCabe answered, "but I won't hold it against you. Now, aren't you glad that I finally talked enough sense into you so that you'd look at it?"

Gideon didn't answer, just continued to stare at the two words that were about to change his life.

McCabe rambled on, seemingly oblivious to the fact that Gideon was undergoing a major life transformation.

"You know you have to take it to the big guy. You have to convince him to let you have this one. You *have* to, Gid. Gid, are you listening to me?"

"What?" He traced the words with the tip of his index finger, feeling the power that they held and the promise of a future that was now within his reach.

"Yes, McCabe, I heard you." Gideon turned and looked fully at his friend, finally gracing him with the smile that everyone at Cupid Headquarters said was a gift from God. "I heard you, and for once I totally agree with you. This *is* my ticket to the big leagues, and I can't screw it up. So go away," he said, turning back to his desk, "so I can figure out the best way to do this."

"No problem," McCabe responded as he headed back to his own desk and the towering pile of RFA forms sitting there. "And you're welcome, winger."

Gideon didn't even respond to the barb, because he was too busy staring once again at the words destined to finally make him a Cupid. There they were, in all their glory . . . his ride to fame, fortune, and acceptance.

So beautiful.

So poetic.

So absolutely perfect.

Two words typed in Times New Roman twelve-point font on cheap-grade copy paper.

Valentine Lewis.

January 7, 2004
Cupid Headquarters
Circle of the Three

"I do not believe he is ready." Eros's words were not loudly spoken, and yet Gideon could hear them from where he was standing outside of the inner sanctum, ear pressed firmly against the wooden door.

He frowned and his hands unconsciously tightened into fists. Eros had to give him this assignment. Had to. It was imperative that he be the Cupid assigned to Valentine's case. Before he could fully prepare himself for a response, he heard another voice.

"He is ready, Your Excellence. He is a good man, Gideon, and he has been studying hard for just such a moment."

Gideon had to smile at his father's voice. He had wondered if Jonathan would defend him, if he had gained enough favor in his father's eyes to bring his request before Eros.

"That may be true, Jonathan, and I have no doubts as to your son's dedication. But you must realize how important this job is, how there can be no missteps in handling it."

Gideon heard Eros's sigh, heard the squeaks and groans that meant the man who ruled the world of love was moving restlessly atop his throne at the head of the table.

Another voice, this time that of Dimitria. She was the only female Cupid, would probably always be the only female allowed into this special world. Gideon knew that it wasn't from prejudice that women were excluded from the job—it was simply the way things worked. The system had been set up this way hundreds of thousands of years ago, and no one would dare to change it now.

"Eros," she said, and a shiver ran down Gideon's spine at her soft, dulcet tones. "There comes a time in every Cupid's life when they reach this moment. A decision has to be made that they are ready, that they know enough, that they are mature enough, to handle important cases. We all realize the highly sensitive nature of the Lewis request. There will be no room for error in judgment on our part, regardless of who is assigned to find her a mate."

Dimitria paused, and with it Gideon held his breath.

"But Gideon has asked for it, and I believe we should grant it to him."

His ear was beginning to throb, pushed painfully into the wood of the door. It was now quiet within the Circle of the Three, and he spent precious moments wondering whether the silence was good or bad.

Eros's voice suddenly reverberated through his body, and he had to pull his ear away from the door to protect his hearing.

"All right then, I will defer to my two consorts in their trust and devotion to Gideon. I will grant him his wish, but I will also hold all three of you accountable if anything goes wrong. You might as well bid him enter, as he's waiting impatiently outside the door, listening with bated breath to our discussion."

The wooden door swung inward, and Gideon's face blushed red with embarrassment at being caught eavesdropping.

"As I assume that you have heard our discussion, Gideon, then you know that I shall grant you your request for the Lewis assignment."

"Yes, Your Excellence."

"That said, I will say only one thing more on the matter. Should you succeed in this quest, you will have no trouble with the rest of your Cupid Exams, or with earning your degree. However, and I can't stress this enough, if there are any complications in this matter, any screwups that require my intervention, you'll be sitting down in Acquisitions as long as I remain the head of the Circle of the Three."

Eros glanced down from his throne, his earnest blue eyes burning into Gideon's brown ones.

"Do I make myself clear?"

Gideon took a deep breath and released it on a rush of air. "Perfectly," he answered, and bowed in deference before he turned to leave.

He paused at the door to glance back at the members of the Council. "I won't mess this up."

In the days that followed, Gideon often thought about how he had felt so confident that day. And how it had all so quickly fallen apart.

TWO

January 11, 2004
Fairview Mall Shopping Plaza

"So, has the man of your dreams shown up on your door-step yet?" There was no malice or ill will in Tasha's voice, but Val heard the sarcasm shining through loud and clear.

"No, not yet. And besides, I'm not sure that's how it works." Val stopped outside the window display at Nord-strom's, eyeing a soft rose cashmere sweater with envy. Then she glanced down at the price tag, and decided she didn't love it that much after all.

Tasha walked up beside her and made a low sound of approval. "Gorgeous, but not that gorgeous."

"Exactly."

They kept walking, no particular destination in mind. About once a month, they made a trip to the mall, to take in the sights and sounds, the shops and sales, and each other's company.

Tasha didn't bring up the Cupid angle again until they were seated in the courtyard, artery-blocking pizza before them on flimsy paper plates.

"You do know that if this works for you, I'll be next in line with a plea."

Val snorted in disbelief. "Since when have you ever needed help in the love life department?"

"Hmm, well never," she answered, licking her lips and trying not to think about how many calories that one bite of supreme had just packed onto her hips. "But, you know, if this works, and you really do find your soul mate, it couldn't hurt for me to ask for a little help."

She took another bite and glanced over at her sister. "Having a good love life doesn't just mean having sex. Granted, I have a lot of sex, too, but I still haven't found the love of my life."

"Don't say that, it makes you sound easy," Val said, laughing.

"Nah, just makes me sound human."

"An easy human."

Tasha loved that they could joke like this, could banter back and forth with the ease of sisterhood and friendship. She had to admit, she thought Val was crazy for trying this Cupid idea. At the same time, though, she had to admit that it took guts. Val knew, after a long dry spell of not knowing, what she wanted. And now she was trying out a system on how to get it. Granted, it was probably the most ridiculous system she'd ever heard of, but who knew, it just might work.

"So." Tasha pushed aside her empty plate and reached for her diet cola. "How do you think this works? Will the person Cupid picks just knock at your door? Or do you think you'll just happen to meet someone, you know, either at work or when you're out at the grocery store one day? And violà! it will be the man you've been waiting for."

Val frowned as she looked down at the table. "I don't know, Tasha, and that's got me a little freaked. I mean, there are two ways that this could go."

"What do you mean?"

"Okay, say that I do meet someone, a guy that I'm really attracted to and who seems to be into me, sometime in the next few weeks. How will I know if this Cupid thing worked, or if it just so happens that it was my time to meet a man?"

"Well, that's a good question. But it seems to me," she answered, taking her sister's hand across the table, "that whether it's fate or Cupid, you'd be happy to have found your one true love. And besides, wouldn't thinking that Cupid set you up with him be a kind of, oh, I don't know, fairy-tale type of idea that you could pull out and look over every once in a while? I mean, come on, just think of the stories you could tell your grandchildren."

Val laughed at her sister's jesting. She was right, the way that she usually was. Tasha might be the younger sister, but in the ways of men and how they worked, she was light-years ahead of her. What did it matter really? If she reached the goal that she'd set for herself, if she found a man who would love her and ultimately be the one that she married, what difference did it make whether it came about due to her own hard work or the hand of Cupid?

"Thanks, sis."

"You're very welcome. Now come on," Tasha said, grabbing her empty lunch dishes to toss them in the trash. "I hear Victoria's Secret calling my name. And if Cupid's due to come calling, she's probably calling your name too."

January 12, 2004
Navy Pier, Chicago

It was amazing to Gideon the masses of people that chose to be outside in this type of weather. It was only twenty-seven degrees, with a brisk wind and only intermittent sunlight peeking through the ominous gray cloud cover. Yet the pier was jam-packed with people: men with long winter coats and briefcases sitting on benches, women with their faces almost completely covered by scarves, going in and out of the shops, and children running and laughing, arguing and yelling, doing all of the things that children do on a blustery winter day.

He'd been here before, of course. Being a Cupid didn't mean he had no life. He actually made his earthly home in Chicago, and Navy Pier never failed to delight him. Its Ferris wheel and carousel, its restaurants, shops, and museums. The promenade was a great place to people-watch, which Gideon loved to do. It was the first time, though, that he'd sought his quarry here.

It was amazing, and made his job a lot easier, that the man he sought lived in Chicago as well. There were seven hubs for Cupids, seven places where they could enter and leave their otherworldly jobs and priorities, in just the United States and Canada alone. New York City, Washington, D.C., Chicago, Las Vegas, Hollywood, Halifax, and Vancouver. Gideon was lucky enough to live in a city where one of the most active Cupid groups was located, but this was the first time that both the person requesting assistance and the person on the receiving end of his help both lived where he did.

Gideon knew who he was looking for. Tyler Morris, an ad exec for one of the most prominent real estate agents in town. The man was good at his job, kept an eye on his finances, looked good in a suit, and had a great sense of humor. Gideon figured that if anyone fit the bill, Tyler was the man.

Man, but the wind was brisk. He pulled up the collar of his coat a little higher and breathed some warmth into his gloved hands. Contrary to popular belief, a Cupid didn't have to wear a toga or anything resembling a large male diaper. Gideon wore normal clothes, especially when he was wandering around on Earth. Thinking over some of the lore that humans had about Cupid had him chuckling.

Cupids existed in a state of being that was hard to comprehend. His father, Jonathan, was a Cupid, an immortal being who was over seven hundred years old. His mother, though, was human, and although she'd been turned immortal by Eros, she still exhibited most of her human ways. She fussed over Gideon like a typical mother, she liked to cook and bake and clean, and she had a healthy dose of ego that made her take a certain kind of pride in her appearance.

Cupids also weren't invisible. Well, not exactly. When they were in working mode, as he was now, he used his cloak of invisibility, something that he had been trained to do in school. It was all a matter of using a certain portion of his mind that most humans weren't aware of and blocking his presence to mortal men. In this state, though, there were still three groups of beings who could see him. Other Cupids, mortal children under the age of two, and for some innately strange reason, cats.

As he took a seat on one of the benches ringing the Ferris wheel, he had to laugh. He really didn't understand the cat thing. Little children, yes, with their innocence and pleasure in life and everything that surrounded them, he could understand. But no one, not even Eros, had ever explained to him why cats could see them when they were invisible to everyone else.

Cupids, obviously, were also not one person. Too much work for one being to make all the matches that were requested of them. Eros was their leader, their lawmaker, their guide and mentor. The god of love had powers that no other Cupid could ever hope to attain, and it suited them just fine. But there were over two thousand Cupids in just the United States, not to mention those operating out of the two hubs in Canada and the other thirty-seven locations throughout the rest of the world.

Gideon let his mind wander as he watched the people pass. He smiled charmingly at a little blond-headed infant who passed by in a stroller, and she gave him back a toothless grin. The wind was still coming off of the Lake, but the sun was out and the resulting shine was kicking up the temperature a few notches.

He glanced around, and finally saw Tyler sitting not fifty feet away from him on another bench.

"Time to get to work."

The actual making of a match wasn't totally unlike what humans thought it was. He did own an arrow, and he would need to use it for the task at hand. The two parties involved didn't have to be in the same spot at the same time; Gideon only had to concentrate on the person not in attendance while performing his duty. He'd gone over Val's dossier once again earlier this morning, and had her pretty cerulean blue eyes and long black hair pictured in his head. Now all that was left was saying the words that would make her request come true, aiming his arrow, and hitting his mark.

Tyler was engrossed in his laptop, undoubtedly scheming up another ad campaign that would have his business selling more houses. The people passing in front of him didn't seem to deter him, but they gave Gideon pause.

He hated shooting through people.

Granted, it did harm neither to the person it passed through nor to his aim, but it always gave him a weird feeling inside. The people he hit couldn't see him, true enough, but he could sure see them, and watching an arrow pass smoothly through their heads, midsection, or legs had a bad effect on his stomach.

Gideon took the bow stationed at his hip and pulled an arrow from the quiver at his back. He chose to go old school when it came to his tool, not yet having given in to the rage of getting a hip quiver. It might have provided easier access, but the feel of it, the smooth motions that it took to grab an arrow by its neck and double-check that the cock-feather was in the correct position—it gave him a sense of purpose, of accomplishment.

He was already wearing the brace on his left arm, and he

removed his leather gloves to steady his grip. Gideon knew that he could have left the gloves on and still hit his mark, but he wanted to feel the sting of the wind, the cold of the air, as he watched the results of his teachings ring true.

Archery was a major part of Cupid training. Actually, as a child of only fifty, his father had enrolled him in archery classes. It was hard to remember exactly how many courses he had taken over the last several decades, how many times he had set an arrow upon the bow and taken aim.

He did so now, waiting for a clear shot. He once again brought the picture of beautiful, stubborn, and oh-so-important Valentine Lewis to mind, and closed his thoughts and ears to all outside stimulation. It was time to prepare the words that would prove his worth to everyone that mattered—to his father, to Dimitria, to Eros, to all of the other Cupids entering training. And most importantly, to himself. Gideon needed to do this, and do it right, to meet the final goal that he'd set for himself so many years ago. Get this done, and do it right, and he'd no longer be a winger. He'd be a Cupid, and a Cupid is the one thing that he'd always needed to be.

The coast was clear. Gideon looked right and left, and seeing no one hurrying in his direction from either way, raised his bow and took aim.

> "With this my arrow
> Strong and true,
> I bind you to her
> And she to you.
> This bond I forge
> No mortal may break.
> This vow of love, I,
> As a Cupid now make."

He felt the release in his arm before he ever let go. Strong and true, just as it needed to be, he watched with a smile upon his face as it took flight toward poor, unsuspecting Tyler Morris. Gideon had to cringe a little, when halfway to its mark, it ran through the shoulder of a boy of about ten who had run into its path, but sighed with relief when the arrow continued on its way.

Then the horrible and unimaginable happened right before his eyes. The wind moaned, a long sigh of frustration, and his arrow moved off target. Gideon shielded his eyes against the sudden glare of the sun reemerging from behind the clouds, as he tried to track the new course his arrow was taking.

Up, down, sideways—he couldn't keep track of the darn thing. And then he lost sight of it completely, and he panicked. Gideon turned, to his left, to his right, behind him. He still couldn't see the damn arrow.

Gideon, son of one of the Circle of the Three. Gideon, the boy who had turned into a man, who was still a winger but well on his way to becoming a full-fledged Cupid. Gideon, of the hundreds upon hundreds of hours of archery training.

His first assignment, the assignment of a lifetime, and he'd blown it. Because suddenly, Gideon knew without a doubt where the arrow had gone. For a moment he just stood there: shock, anger, grief, embarrassment all warring within him.

Then he gave in to what had to be the worst of really bad days and reached behind him. Gideon grasped the neck of his arrow, and pulled. And then he simply sat down, right there in the middle of the promenade, as he contemplated what the ramifications had to be for a Cupid who shot himself in the ass.

January 12, 2004
Eros's Private Chambers

Eros sat alone in his drawing room, a roaring fire in the marble-lined fireplace and a glass of thirty-year-old sherry in his hand. The book he had been reading sat forgotten on the table by his chair as he ran a weary hand through his head of silver hair.

His cat, Agape, yawned and stretched on the jewel-toned footstool to his right. The cat's eyes glowed a pale yellow in the light from the fire as he turned his head to stare at his owner. The thoughts tumbled from Agape's mind like pebbles over a calm body of water, making their way without words into Eros's consciousness.

"Yes, my dear feline, the boy has definitely made a mess of things."

The god of love took another sip of his sherry and sighed, both in contentment at the warm, pleasurable feeling of the liquor and at the problem that now lay heavy upon his mind. He felt the cat's thoughts take a turn in another direction and had to laugh.

"Agape, you rascal, you alone would find the humor in a Cupid shooting himself in the posterior." Another sigh, one of weariness at yet another crisis he would be required to handle. "The fact is," he interrupted his pet, "such a situation has never occurred before. I have to admit that I'm at a loss on how to handle it."

Again his trusted advisor had thoughts on the matter.

"Hmm, well yes, I suppose you're right. But you do realize, dear sir, that although a Cupid's arrow has no effect on a Cupid without my say-so, Gideon isn't yet a Cupid. He's still in training, hasn't yet passed his Final Exams. That worries me. I have a distinct feeling that our Gideon is going to suffer some consequences that I've never considered."

Eros had to smile at his friend's meow of protest. "I didn't say it would be insurmountable. I just said that I have never considered the effects if such a situation ever did occur.

"I suppose, Agape, that you and I will just have to watch the events unfold together. Hopefully, given the sensitive and highly important nature of this particular match, our boy will be able to pull it off. We'll work on the individual plights and pains as they arise."

He stretched his legs before the fire and finished his nightly sherry. "Actually, Gideon and his bad aim just might provide us with a bit of amusement. Granted, I will not, of course, be able to be anything but stern with Dimitria and Jonathan, since it was at their urging that I assigned Gideon to Valentine Lewis."

Eros rose and removed his robe, moving to pull back the quilts from his bed. "But if this works out favorably in the end, I'll be the first to congratulate them on their foresight."

The cat's brain continued to churn and roil, but Eros shut it out with little difficulty. *Cats*, he thought as he drifted off to sleep, *could by some be considered the bane of creation.*

Three

January 14, 2004
Gideon's House, Chicago

He hadn't gone to work for two days. It was a cowardly act, and he knew it, but he didn't go just the same. Instead, Gideon was still lying in bed, the covers twisted around his naked body, staring moodily at the ceiling of the house he called his own.

Eros had to know by now what had happened. Just as he undoubtedly knew the reason he hadn't shown up for work yesterday or today.

Gideon sighed and rolled over, bunching the pillow into a more comfortable position. It was pathetic really, to still be lying in bed at two in the afternoon. But what else was there for him to do? He'd screwed up and he was too scared to face the consequences of his actions. Call him what you wanted, but he valued his life.

Sleep. Just a few more hours of sleep, and he'd get up and shower, dress, and drink a pot of coffee. Then he'd think about, and worry about, what to do next. He'd think up a plan and how best to finagle his way out of what was quickly turning into a major train wreck of a disaster.

A few more hours of peaceful, dreamless sleep was all that he needed. A sleep free from the pictures of Valentine's face, of her blue eyes and black hair, of her long legs and perky breasts. For some reason, he couldn't get Val out of his mind, and it was driving him crazy, especially the perky breasts part.

When he finally slept, he dreamt of her.

Gideon was back at Navy Pier, except this time the sun was warm on his face and the air was tinted with the smells of summer. Cotton candy, corn dogs, and the scent of too many sweaty children in one place drifted on the air.

He stopped before the carousel, smiling at the brilliant colors of the ponies and lions, the carriages and mythical creatures that passed before him, around and around again. A scream tore through the air, but it was the scream of excitement, of exuberance, instead of one of terror.

Gideon chose a seat on a bench facing the carousel, so that he could continue to watch the circling of the ride, the never-ending line of children and their parents, and hear the calliope music that filtered through the noise.

He looked down and realized that in his hand he held a cone of cotton candy, pink and fluffy and looking like the epitome of summer. There was nothing like summer at the Pier, he thought to himself. The only thing missing was the woman he loved, and somehow he knew that she would be along shortly.

Gideon glanced to his left as he sensed a slight movement, a small variation in the space surrounding him. A brilliant smile lit his face as he saw her, the woman who made his life complete. He watched in awe, in amazement, as this beautiful woman who loved him back took his hand and sat beside him.

They didn't speak. It was enough for Gideon to sit in the warm sunshine and hold her hand. It seemed to heat his own hand, infuse it with a warm glow, and in a perfect moment of clarity he watched as he pulled her hand to his lips and placed a kiss in her palm. The miracle of finding her was a daily surprise, a surprise that he thanked the powers-that-be for each and every morning.

A little boy passed before them, pulling his father along in a trot as he almost hopped his way to the carousel.

"C'mon, Dad, c'mon! I wanna ride it one more time, Dad, okay? Just one more time, and this time I wanna ride the unicorn. Can I ride the unicorn, Dad?"

The father's laughter added to Gideon's joy as he watched the man run a hand through the boy's hair. Such love, such affection. A part of him, a part deep inside his heart, his soul, filled with longing. To have a child like that someday, he thought, and turned to his love with an unasked question on his lips. But she knew, somehow, what he wanted to say, what he wished to ask. And she smiled a gorgeous smile that lit up her eyes and made them even bluer. She reached to push a lock of her long black hair away from her face, and she answered his silent question.

"One day, Gideon, one day."

And his heart filled almost to bursting as he realized that Valentine Lewis, the woman he'd waited a lifetime to find, would one day bear his child. Eros had to be smiling on him today.

But suddenly Val was gone, and so were the carousel and the sweet smells of summer. He was no longer on the Pier, but inside the chamber that contained the Circle of the Three. Dimitria was speaking, and she was very—what was the word—peeved. His own father sat, still as a statue, as he kept his eyes downcast upon the marble desk before him. And Eros—Eros had a look of dignified horror upon his face, a look that Gideon had never seen before.

He didn't understand why he was here, what he had done to make them so upset. And why were all of the other Cupids here, even the other Cupids-in-training like him? There were hundreds of them, thousands, in the gallery, up on the balcony. Why was he here? He had no idea what was *going on. Until he went to sit down in the offered chair, and realized that he had an arrow protruding from his body.*

An arrow—sticking out of his butt.

Gideon awoke, shaking and cursing, the cries of "winger" still reverberating in his head as he tried to remember what he had just dreamt, what it could mean. He couldn't wrap his mind around the details, couldn't seem to recall exactly where he had been or what he had been doing.

All he knew was that Val had been there, and that she had loved him. And that he had loved her, more than he'd ever loved anything in his life.

And that there had been, once again, an arrow stuck in a place where an arrow should never have to be.

He gave up on the idea of taking a shower and drinking some coffee. Instead, he buried his head under his pillow, pulled the blanket up and around him like a cocoon, and thought about screaming until he passed out.

January 14, 2004
Lehman-Altman Accounting Firm

It was turning out to be one of those days. The kind that start off badly, steadily progress to worse, and ultimately end up at "please, someone shoot me now."

Val had overslept. She had no idea how it had happened, either. She'd gone to bed at eleven, like she almost always did. She'd set her alarm for six-thirty to make it to work promptly at eight. And yet somehow she'd woken up, torn from a dream about a man with golden hair and chocolate brown eyes, to the tune of a squawking alarm clock that flashed eight thirty-five in bright red numerals.

She flew through the morning ritual of a shower and blow-dry, even skipping that holy routine of slathering moisturizer on her skin to keep it from drying out in the winter weather. Hair pulled back in a quick ponytail, a swipe of mascara and lip gloss, and she was ready to go.

But then there was the car. Her trusty, reliable old monstrosity that, although it looked like something from a Stephen King novel, still got her to and from where she needed to go each day. Except, of course, for today. Old reliable decided that seventeen degrees, with a wind-chill below zero, was just too damn cold to get moving. So Val sat, talking and pleading and finally crying, in freezing temperatures while she bargained with her car to start. Before she knew it, twenty minutes had passed, her fingers were numb even through the leather of her gloves, and the snot from her crying jag had frozen.

Needless to say, neither she nor the driver of the cab she finally called was in a particularly good mood when they pulled up outside the offices of Lehman-Altman.

It proved to get even better. The account she'd been working on for days, for hundreds of man-hours, was sitting on her desk when she finally sat down at almost ten o'clock. Along with it was a note—and not one of those "thanks for the great job" types either. Oh, no. This note was full of snipes, full of lines marked with the dreaded yellow highlighter. Seems Mr. Allen had changed his mind a couple of hundred times about exactly how he wanted this particular account handled, and it was now up to her to re-align not only her thinking, but the entire job that she'd spent better than a week tweaking to perfection.

Val worked hard for over four hours, flipping through her notes, pulling up pertinent information on her computer, typing and retyping documents that were already in their fifth or sixth draft. Finally though, at almost two-thirty, she called it quits and decided to take her lunch break. She'd skipped breakfast in her bid to get to work no later than she had to, and the resulting growls of her stomach had her twitching.

The cafeteria in the office complex was blessedly calm and quiet. The lunch rush hit at noon and she'd avoided it skillfully. Only a handful of people sat at the multitude of tables, and after Val went through the line, picking up a salad and a cola, she chose a solitary spot in the corner of the room.

"Peace. Just fifteen minutes of blessed, wonderful peace."

It was a prayer of sorts, that she would enjoy her lunch alone and with nothing but her thoughts to amuse her. She dug into the salad, liberally topped with high-calorie blue cheese dressing, and proceeded to inhale with delight. Val had always enjoyed food—the textures, the taste, the resulting good feeling that it left her with. Tasha was always concerned with fat grams and carbs, and Val didn't understand it. Her sister was actually in great shape, although Tasha didn't think so. She was always talking about the five pounds she wanted to lose, and she had the tenacity and willpower to stick to her guns when it came to food.

But Val, on the other hand, loved food. It was a good thing that she had a very high metabolism, a system that seemed to burn off fat as fast as she consumed it. She was five foot nine, an Amazon in the world of modern-day women, but she weighed only a hundred and thirty pounds. A lean, mean, eating machine. Her momma always said that she was a long, cool drink of water. The thought made her smile. And remember that she hadn't talked to her parents for almost two weeks, a situation that she would rectify this evening.

After a nice long bath and a glass of wine. Or maybe two.

Val saw him then, sitting alone at a table across the room, a newspaper in front of him. Her heart did a little tap dance inside her chest, and the bite of salad she'd just taken got stuck on its way down.

Good Lord, but the man was handsome.

Short hair the color of chestnuts seemed to shine in the light, and even from fifty feet away she could see the intense emerald green of his eyes. His fingers were idly tapping to a tune on the top of the table, and Val noticed that they were long and solid-looking.

She sighed. She'd always had a thing for nice hands. And gorgeous eyes. And a nice, tight butt.

"Easy, Tonto," she whispered to herself. She took another sip of cola and then the thought hit her, right in the belly which was doing a few little twists and turns from the view.

What if this was the one? The one that Cupid had sent her? Crap, what should she do?

She watched him out of the corner of her eye as she finished her salad. Criminy, but the man looked good. Even as he was, casual and at rest, just reading the paper and finishing his coffee, he looked good. Part of Val hoped that he was the one Cupid had sent. Good-looking, in an easy yet polished sort of way. He obviously had a good job, or he wouldn't be dressed in the suit that he was, or even work in this building. And his hands. Val sighed again as she thought of those long, slender fingers—and the things that such fingers could do to a woman.

Unfortunately, her fantasy was shattered within the next few minutes, as she watched Mr. Heartthrob pick his teeth with a piece of paper he tore off from the one in front of him. As her stomach did a little dip in rebuttal, said cutey then proceeded to let out a caffeine-induced burp as he pushed away from the table. And to top it all off, to the chagrin of both her libido and her tidy, orderly brain, he didn't even bother to take his lunch dishes to the trash before he sauntered out the door. Sauntered, she noticed, while scratching a part of his anatomy that really, *really* shouldn't be scratched in public.

Val just laid her head on the table in defeat.

"If this is the best you can do, then I'm in serious trouble."

She stayed at work until almost seven, finishing up the

Stevenson portfolio. Val was tempted to draw a stick-man with a dagger through his heart on the note she left for Mr. Allen, but in the end decided to just write "done" on it and leave it at that.

It wasn't until she was halfway to the parking garage that she remembered she'd had to take a cab to work.

"Why, oh why, does my life so totally *suck?*" She almost sobbed it, but her pride and dignity kept her from really belting out another crying spell. Instead, she tromped back into the office and asked security to call her a cab.

When she finally got home, she didn't even bother with her evening routine of checking her answering machine and taking something out for dinner. Val opened the refrigerator and with one hand grabbed her bottle of Pinot Grigio that she'd been saving for a special occasion. Turning around, she opened a cabinet and snagged a wineglass, dropping her coat and gloves on the floor on the way to the bathroom.

She set the bottle of wine and the glass on the sink, then drew a bath with water as hot as she could stand it. Pouring in a generous amount of her favorite mango bath gel, she poured a glass of wine and downed it in one long swallow.

Glass refilled and in hand, she walked back into the living room to her CD player. She needed music—something fast and pumping to get her out of her funk. Val flipped through her CDs, finally settling on one by Madonna. Good old Madonna, the stand-by music she could always count on.

As "Papa Don't Preach" blared out of her speakers, she took another long swallow of wine and peeled her clothes off on the way back to her bath. She did a little jig along with the beat, filled her glass to the rim, and gratefully sank into the hot water.

A half an hour later she woke up to water that had cooled considerably and her glass floating on top of the now milky water. Her hands and feet were wrinkled, but she was definitely more relaxed. Her music had stopped, sometime after she'd last been singing along to "Like a Virgin."

Val took the time now to rub herself with tropical fruit moisturizer, then wrapped herself up in her favorite purple robe.

The knock on her door as she was heating up a frozen dinner was unexpected, and annoying. She didn't want to talk to anyone, not now, maybe not for a few days. But it could be Tasha, and if it was, Val knew that she'd have a willing ally in her upcoming rant against men and life in general.

The microwave dinged as she took one more drink of wine, carrying the glass with her as she went to the door. The bell had rung again while she had been debating whether to answer it or not.

Thank God I answered it was her first thought as the door swung open and her eyes adjusted to the brightness of her hallway.

He was perfection, utter perfection in male form. Near-shoulder-length hair, a shade of blond that she'd never seen before and had no name for. And eyes the color of melted chocolate, like perfect ovals of the Godiva she stashed away in her emergency chocolate drawer.

It took her a minute to realize that she'd seen him somewhere before, that somehow she knew him. And it hit her that this was the man she'd dreamed of last night, before the start of her really shitty day; she didn't even realize that she'd loosened her hold on the wineglass until she felt the liquid splash against her bare feet.

Val looked down to see wine making a hideous-looking stain on her gray carpet and growled low in her throat, forgetting for a moment the man still standing in her doorway.

But then he stepped over the threshold, picked up the fallen glass, and stared directly into her soul. At least that's what it felt like, and when she looked into those brown eyes, when she felt him brush lightly against her arm and the resulting zap that zinged its way through her body, she knew that there was no way on earth she'd ever forget him again.

Four

Gideon wasn't sure what he was going to say until the words just popped out of his mouth.

"You're even more beautiful than I thought you'd be."

His heart had done a somersault inside his chest when she'd opened the door. The blood had rushed to his head, making him a little dizzy. It had also pooled in a part of his body that he'd long ago thought was tamed.

Obviously not.

Val had backed up a step, one hand automatically taking the wineglass from him and the other going to her throat as she bunched the lapels of her robe in one fist. She was staring at him now as if he was either a threat to her security or a figment of her imagination.

Maybe he was both.

"I'm sorry. I didn't mean to startle you. I was wondering if we could talk."

Gideon watched as color simultaneously gathered in her cheeks and drained away from the rest of her face. She backed up another step, loosening her hold on her robe to thrust her hands out before her. To ward him off.

"I don't know you. Yes, I do. No, no. No, I don't," she mumbled, making pushing motions at him with her hands. "Go away. Why would I want to talk to you? I don't know you."

He was sorry for her confusion, but it didn't calm the racing of his heart or the throbbing in his loins.

"I'm sorry. Really. But it's very important that I talk to you."

Val was shaking her head now, taking small steps backward and wildly glancing around at anything but him. "But I don't know you. I mean, you're not here. I'm dreaming." She finally stopped backing away and looked up into his face. "That's it. I fell asleep in the bathtub, and this is all just another dream."

Gideon smiled. Denial. He could handle denial.

"You're not dreaming, luv. My name is Gideon, and it's very important that we talk."

She just stood there shaking her head at him. "This is insane. Totally insane. A man I don't know is standing inside my door, telling me we need to talk."

She was talking to herself. It was starting to worry him. Next would come panic, and he didn't know if he could handle panic.

"Look, luv, I'm just going to back out into the hallway. See?" Gideon took a few steps back until the threshold stood between them. "How about I go downstairs to the lobby and you can come down and we'll talk?"

It seemed that denial and panic moved quickly into anger. Val rushed the door, and with one swing he watched as it edged toward his face. The slam reverberated through the hallway.

He sighed. Women. He didn't have much experience in handling women, and this one was proving to be more trying than most.

Gideon rang the doorbell. He could feel the weight of her stare through the peephole.

"Go away."

Her voice was muffled but firm through the solid wood of the door.

"I can't."

She was still there, on the other side, and Gideon swore he could almost hear her moaning in frustration.

He was going to have to do something, say something, that he would have preferred to wait and say until she was calmer. Until she was more ready to hear it. No time for waiting now, though, or he'd never get her out of her apartment.

"Val, it's about the Cupid thing."

Her sharp intake of breath was loud enough for him to hear through four inches of solid door.

"I don't know what you're talking about."

Although her voice was low-pitched, he heard the sharp thread of uncertainty that laced it.

"I'm going downstairs now, Val. I'll wait for you there."

Gideon had no choice. She'd either come down or she wouldn't. If she did, then he'd explain to her as quickly and as calmly as he could what was going on. And if she didn't . . . well, if she didn't, he'd just have to come back up here and hound her until she opened the door again.

She was either hallucinating, suffering a nervous breakdown, or about to depart on a ride that wasn't based on factual scientific knowledge. Regardless of which one it turned out to be, the words "Cupid thing" kept clamoring around in her head like a ship on a very angry sea.

Val was sitting on the floor in the puddle of wine right inside her front door. The man . . . Gideon, she reminded herself . . . had left. Presumably he was waiting in the lobby for her. But she could still see the sexy tumble of his golden hair, the sensual tint of his brown eyes, like a photograph frozen behind her eyes.

It was happening. Everything she'd asked for, hoped for, was happening, and she was in no way ready for it. Val hadn't expected a real live person to show up at her door talking about Cupid and arrows and love. She hadn't expected . . . well, anything. She didn't know what she had anticipated when she'd written that letter asking for help, but she knew without a doubt that this wasn't it.

It was time to act. She wouldn't, couldn't, just sit here with wine seeping into her best robe and pout about not being ready. Valentine Lewis was a woman of action, and if ever a time called for action, this would be it.

Val jumped up and rushed to the kitchen, grabbing a dishrag to clean up the wine from her living room floor. Task accomplished, she needed to change. What should she wear? What did you wear when you talked to someone wanting to discuss Cupid? She finally settled on jeans and a sapphire blue turtleneck sweater that brought out the color of her eyes.

There was no need to be anything less than impressive.

She slipped on a pair of black flats, grabbed her purse, and headed out to meet her destiny.

Val paused for a moment as she reached the lobby and just looked at him. Gideon. She had to keep reminding herself that although she as yet had no idea what he would tell her, the man had a name.

It seemed to fit him. Gideon reminded her of angels, and the man sure as heck looked like one. That hair, those eyes, the smile. He looked good. Very good. Good in a hormonal surge, sexy sort of way. A part of her was depressed at the thought that if he was here about her letter, then he wasn't the man she was intended to fall in love with. The thought made her a little sad.

He was sitting on one of the couches near the palm trees. The owners of the complex had tried, and failed miserably, to make the lobby take on the appearance of a charming, exciting tropical oasis. Fake palm trees, apricot-colored couches and chairs, and monkeys hanging from strings, however, did not a tropical paradise make.

A large indrawn breath to still her raging heart, a quick

prayer to whoever was listening for courage, and Val approached him. His smile was quick and genuine, and it lit up his entire face. The man had a mouth to die for.

She sat down quickly in a chair across from him, afraid that if she kept standing much longer her legs would turn completely to jelly and she'd just collapse into a quivering pile of need in front of him.

"Well." She didn't know what else to say. The man had, after all, come to her, so he should be the one to get this show on the road.

"Yes. Well. Now that you're here, I hardly know where to start."

He was very calm about it, but she noticed that his hands were shaking just a bit. Beautiful hands, she noticed, and pushed the thought away. She'd had enough thoughts about hands and skillful fingers for one day.

"Just spit it out, sir . . . umm, Gideon. Just say what you need to say, and we'll take it from there. Obviously, I want to hear it, or I'd still be upstairs."

"True enough. It's just that, well, what I have to talk to you about isn't the easiest thing I've ever had to say."

He was squirming now, and it made her unbelievably nervous. Val fought hard to avoid doing the same in her own seat, and concentrated instead on the man across from her.

"For God's sake, just tell me already. The waiting has got to be worse than whatever you have to say."

Val swore that he murmured "I doubt it" under his breath, and it really, *really* didn't make her feel better about the whole thing.

"Yes, okay, I'll just spit it out, as you put it. As I mentioned earlier, my name is Gideon, and I need to talk to you about the request you made to Cupid. See, the fact is, I am a Cupid."

A Cupid? *A* Cupid? Didn't that imply that there were more than one?

Val sat forward on her chair and leaned her head in her hands. This was getting crazier by the minute.

"All right, a Cupid. I'm inferring that you mean there are more than one of you."

"Oh yes, quite a few more. Thousands, in fact." He stopped abruptly, and she guessed that it was in deference to the squeak that had escaped from her throat.

"I'm sorry, I'm sorry. I'm not trying to shock you, really, it's just that I think it's better if I get everything out into the open now, so we can decide what path we want to take once you know why I'm here."

"Well then tell me why *are* you here."

She heard him sigh, and he scooted forward on the couch until their knees were almost touching. Val smelled something light and tangy, his aftershave no doubt. His eyes were intense and focused as he settled his gaze on her own.

"The truth is, we received your request for a love. It was a very important request to us, and I was honored to be assigned to carry it out. But then there were, how to put this, complications."

"What type of complications?"

Val watched as heat gathered steam in his neck and worked its way up into his face. She had a distinct feeling that whatever came next wasn't going to be something she wanted to hear. At all. Ever.

Gideon cleared his throat, and she involuntarily held her breath. "The thing is, I had someone lined up for you. I was there, in his presence, and was all set to go. I won't bother you with the details of how we do it right now, but let's just say that all of the movies and books aren't completely wrong when they depict us with a bow and arrow.

"Anyway, I attempted to make the match, and then something happened, and, well, everything went to hell in a handbasket."

Her eyes narrowed as she looked at him, and even the sorrowful look in those perfect brown eyes couldn't keep down her temper.

"Exactly what sort of complication are we talking about, Gideon?"

"Umm, well, the thing is, I . . . oh, to hell with it." He took a deep breath and grasped her hands in his own. "I shot myself with my own arrow."

Val felt her jaw drop, and heard what she swore was a great gust of wind sweep through the lobby of her building. There was a buzzing in her ears, and she thought for just a moment that, for the first time in her life, she was going to pass out.

"You shot yourself? With an arrow meant for the person who was supposed to be my soul mate?" Surely the voice coming out of her throat wasn't her own. This one was thin and reedy and held more than a small dose of panic.

Gideon cleared his throat and looked away from her. "Yes, that just about sums it up."

The blazing fire of her temper flared up with no conscious thought, and she focused it upon the only person available to her. She was on her feet before she knew it, and she knew that she had to look a whole lot like her mother, eyes burning, hands shaking as she held them on her hips.

"You're going to sit there and tell me that you were supposed to find me someone to spend my life with and instead you shot *yourself*? What are you, a total idiot? Did you lose your personal copy of *Cupid for Dummies*?"

"Now wait just a minute," he interrupted, and Val could see that she'd pissed him off.

Good, she thought, he can be just as irritated and mad as I am.

"No, buddy, *you* wait a minute! I wrote that letter to Cupid, or to all the Cupids, or to whomever so I could get some help. So that you guys could do a better job of finding me someone than I've so far done for myself. So here you are, raring to go, and what do you do but shoot yourself instead of the target."

Val was practically yelling now, and she had to work hard to lower her voice. Gideon was standing in front of her, his hands waving and his face burning. A part of her almost felt sorry for him, but then she reminded herself what a piss-poor job he'd done and she worked herself up all over again.

"So you shot yourself, and now my chances of getting any help in finding love are shot into the next solar system. Good job, Gideon, thanks for your help. Thanks for *nothing*. At least on my own I could bother to get my aim straight."

"Wait, wait, would you please just take a deep breath and listen to me?"

"Why? So you can tell me some more about how a Cupid shot himself on assignment? I think I've heard enough, thank you very much."

He made a pleading sound in his throat, but she was in no mood to listen to it. Or him.

"Just go away. Go far, far away, before I do something totally unlike me and slap that pretty face of yours. I think I'd better take it from here, don't you think?" She started to stomp off, but had one last dart to throw at him on her way out. "Maybe you should try some archery lessons."

Gideon stood still, watching her slam her way into the elevator.

"Well, that didn't go exactly as I'd planned."

Then again, most everything he'd planned regarding Valentine Lewis hadn't stayed on course. He ran his hands through his already mussed hair and closed his eyes for a moment of peace.

He hadn't told her the rest of it. She hadn't given him a chance. Somehow, sometime soon, he needed to tell her the bad news. As if the rest wasn't bad enough.

Valentine Lewis was now the love of his life, and he was hers. He wondered how long it would take her to figure it out.

Five

She was furious. Three days later and she was still madder than she'd ever been in her life.

The nerve. The total nerve of that man, that, that Cupid, to screw up something so important. She still couldn't believe that he'd messed up so totally, so badly, and ruined the last chance she'd had.

Val hadn't even been able to tell Tasha. She'd always told her sister everything, shared the highs and lows of her life with her. Tasha was her best friend, her confidante, her co-defender in the fight against the injustices of the world.

If ever there had been a major injustice, this had to be the mother of them all.

But Val hadn't been able to tell her. Whether it was because she felt stupid, because that damn Cupid was stupid, or just because she didn't feel like crying on her sister's shoulder, she'd kept this mess to herself.

Just rethinking it had her temper threatening to boil over once again. The horrible thing of it was, as angry as she'd been and still was, she couldn't stop thinking about him. Gideon.

When she went to sleep at night, he was there, taunting her in her dreams. When she was at work, supposedly focusing on her latest portfolio, his face would pop into the forefront of her brain. And when she was at home, alone as always, her mind would drift away to thoughts of the man with cocoa eyes and long, slender fingers.

That infuriated her even more.

She lifted the margarita, her second one of the evening, and downed what remained in one long swallow. Val had come to nurse her emotional wounds at Trinity's, a bar and grille that she usually loved and found enjoyable. Tonight, the noise was like a nail driving deep into her skull, but she ignored it. This was her night—to forget about the last couple of days, to forget about work, to forget about the sorry state of affairs that her life was currently in.

To just forget.

Raising her hand to catch the attention of the waitress, she ordered another margarita. They went down smooth, and she wouldn't notice any real effects until she stood up. Ergo . . . she just wouldn't stand up until she had to.

She'd taken a small booth at the back on the bar side. Val felt hidden there, protected, and she didn't have to look or speak to anyone unless she wanted to. Right now, she didn't want to. And she was close to the bar, which tonight was a plus.

Val paid the waitress and tipped generously, as her parents had taught her to do. You reward good service, and her past jobs as a waitress had left her with an instilled value of rewarding well.

It wasn't until she was licking the salt off the rim of her glass that she looked up into the mirror over the bar—and saw her nemesis.

The salt made her choke, and she had to guzzle her drink

like a seasoned pro to stop the hacking. The tequila hit her hard, but not nearly as hard as the brown eyes that were boring into hers through the mirror's reflection.

How dare he enter her private space? This night was for her, damn it, not him. She didn't want to see him. Didn't want to talk to him. Didn't want to look in his eyes and feel her stomach doing the jitterbug dance that she knew it would do.

Fate wasn't cooperating with her. Then again, in the last month, when had fate done anything but sit back on its haunches and laugh its fool head off at her?

Gideon sat down in the booth across from her, and she didn't say a word. She couldn't. Her mind was frozen, her tongue a useless object taking up space in her mouth. God, she hoped this sudden paralysis was temporary.

"I think I'm falling in love with you."

It was the last thing she'd expected him to say, and it was her undoing. Tears leaked out from under her lids, and she further humiliated herself by choking out a sob.

Stress. She was under too much stress and she'd finally snapped. That had to be it. Val Lewis, of the February birthday and romantic name, did not burst into tears at the insane ramblings of a good-looking man.

No matter how many margaritas she'd had to drink.

By magic it seemed, he produced a handkerchief from the pocket of his burgundy-colored leather jacket, and passed it across the table to her.

"You are the craziest person I've ever met," she told him around the hankie. Val wiped her eyes and blew her nose, then simply sat and stared at him.

Falling in love with her. He was certifiably insane. He didn't even know her. He'd only met her three days ago. Oh, and not to mention he was a Cupid!

Tears threatened to spill again, but she gathered her strength and held them back. There would be no more crying or feeling sorry for herself. She had a psycho Cupid on her hands, and it was going to take everything she had to rid herself of him.

"You need to go away and leave me alone." There. That had sounded forceful, and almost like she had meant it.

"I can't."

Val grit her teeth and tore her napkin into strips as she glared at him. "You know, for a Cupid, there sure seems to be a whole hell of a lot you can't do. Like aim, for instance."

Pain crossed Gideon's face, and a sharp poke of something jabbed her in the gut. She was never mean. Oh, she was sarcastic, and mouthy, but she was never downright mean. Her conscience was giving her grief over hurting this man, and Val knew that her conscience had every reason to do it.

"I'm sorry." And she was. No matter how angry she was, or how angry she was going to be, hurting Gideon wasn't an option. At least not one she could live with. "I'm letting my temper get the best of me, and it's making me nasty. I'm not usually nasty, Gideon, and I apologize."

"I can't say that it's not well deserved."

"Maybe not. But there's still no reason for it. Since you're here, I'm guessing that we still have things to discuss, and it would benefit both of us if I forget the sarcastic barbs and act like a decent human being while we're doing it."

"I appreciate it. Both the fact that you're thinking of my feelings, and that you're willing to listen to what I have to say."

Val glanced around for the waitress, needing more fortification for the task ahead. "I don't really know that I have a choice," she said to him.

His sigh was either one of frustration or regret, but he kept his cool. "No, Val, I guess there are a lot of things that aren't really in our hands anymore."

What did that mean? Oh God, she didn't even want to know what that meant.

The drink arrived, the transaction was made, and Val was left alone in the company of a Cupid. The jury was still out on how she felt about that.

"Maybe you could just say whatever it is you still need to say. Then we can both just go our separate ways and this can be done."

Gideon's smile this time was gentle. "There's the kicker, luv. No matter what I say, no matter how we both feel, we can't just go our separate ways."

Margarita-induced buzz be damned. She had to stand up, had to get away, and she had to do it now.

Frustration was wearing his nerves thin. No matter what he said to Val, no matter how he tried to say it, everything freaked her out. He couldn't comprehend it, and maybe that was part of the problem.

The woman had, after all, written a plea to Cupid asking for help. That showed that she at least had an inkling that there were things out there that science couldn't define. Some things not of this world, things greater than she could see. But now that it was here, staring her in the face, poor Val was having a hard time accepting it.

A large part of him felt sorry for her, sorry for the situation he'd gotten them both into. Another part, though, felt giddy and joyous knowing that, although it was an accident, he was now in love with Valentine. And soon, whether she wanted to admit it or not, she'd be in love with him.

Gideon hadn't known how things would work out. He'd gone to Eros two days ago, admitting his already well-known transgression and seeking his leader's advice. It had worried him that Eros hadn't had that much advice to give. Seems that no other Cupid—ever—had shot himself with an arrow in the midst of an assignment.

This was new territory, for him, for Val, for the god of love.

Not really the way he'd planned on starting his career,

but he could deal with it. He had no choice. That arrow had changed his life's course, had changed Val's, and now all they could do was work with what they had.

He wanted a beer. It was an urge that was totally unexpected and slightly scary. Gideon had never tasted alcoholic beverages; he'd never had the urge to try one. Sitting in the back of Trinity's, with Val in the rest room and nothing to do but listen to the voices around him, the thirst for a beer was so strong that it was like a physical ache in his chest.

Sort of like the ache he'd had for Val ever since he'd seen her three nights ago.

Gideon went to the bar and ordered a beer, then drank half of it leaning against the counter. Cold, refreshing. It went down quite well, and he took the bottle back to the booth with him. Now he knew why humans drank so much of it.

Back to Val . . . and that ache. Since the first moment he'd laid eyes on her, he'd wanted to touch her, kiss her. Her hair was a long fall of black down across her shoulders almost to her waist. Her eyes, the prettiest, clearest blue he'd ever seen, showed so much of her feelings and emotions each time he looked into them.

And her lips were to die for. He'd gladly give up, well, something, to taste those lips with his own. If nothing else came of this night, if nothing else got settled, he promised himself that he'd at least get one sip of what she tasted like.

Sensing movement beside him, he turned to see her slide back into the booth. She looked a little calmer now, though she was pale. He wondered briefly if she'd been sick.

"Are you okay?"

Those clear blue eyes met his dark brown ones and she managed a lopsided grin. "Okay? No, not really. But I'm guessing that I'll survive."

"I surely hope so."

Val placed her hands palms down on the table and met his gaze. "Let's just get this taken care of and we'll decide where to go from there. You should probably start."

It was batter up, and Gideon was next to the plate.

Please don't let me screw this up.

He took another swallow of his beer and took her hand. He felt her pulse jump but she didn't pull away, and he took that as a good sign.

"I'll start at the beginning the best that I can. There are so many things to say, to tell you, that I'm hoping I don't get everything jumbled up. If you have any questions, just ask me. We're in this together now, Val, you and I, so just ask me, all right?"

At her nod of assent he continued.

"You have to understand that we receive hundreds of requests a day. Sometimes it's thousands. And no, we don't honor them all."

Val cocked an eyebrow at him and he had to laugh.

"There are still some things that people need to do for themselves. A lot of people ask us to find them a mate without having first done any work on their own. If you don't try to find true love by yourself, how can you ask someone else to do it for you?"

"Good point. Keep going."

"Okay. Anyway, the number of requests that we actually process varies day by day. It's a long, tedious process that I won't bore you with. Let's just say that when it comes right down to it, we only actually take on about ten percent of the cases that we receive."

Val smiled at him. "You're the last-ditch hope, just like I thought."

"In technical terms I guess that's just about right. So when we received your request, everyone at Headquarters was very excited—and very anxious that it be done right."

"Why? What's so important about me and my request?"

Gideon frowned. He needed to step lightly here, or Val and her temper were going to take off like a rocket ship.

"We have a list. A list of people who are the least likely to ever ask us for assistance. A list of five hundred people, throughout the world, that aren't used to asking for help, especially from something as insane sounding as Cupid."

"But what does that have to do with me?"

"Val, you're number three on the list."

He watched as her mouth formed an "O" of surprise, or maybe outrage, and braced himself for the coming attack.

Thankfully, it never came, but the solitary tear that leaked from the corner of her stormy blue eyes totally undid him.

"Oh man, Val, don't cry. Please, don't cry." Tears of outrage he could handle. A woman pissed off he could deal with. But Gideon had no clue how to handle the sadness of a woman like Val—a beautiful woman who did things to his libido that had never been done before.

Val simply lowered her head until her ebony hair covered her face like a curtain. She didn't make a sound, but he knew the tears continued to fall.

He sat there, not knowing what to do, not knowing what to say, until he finally did the one thing he'd wanted to do since he first saw her. He reached across the table and lifted her chin with his hand. Tears were still wet on her cheeks, so he used the pads of his fingers to wipe them away.

Then he simply leaned over and kissed her.

Val didn't know what had brought the tears on. She didn't cry like this, not Val, woman warrior, defender of women everywhere. But somehow, knowing that she was third on a list of people that even the god of love thought pathetic was her undoing.

The tears were forgotten when Gideon's lips met her own.

Her first thought was "wow." Her second was that there was no way a Cupid should be able to kiss like that. Then there were no more thoughts as her brain went fuzzy and her stomach began doing somersaults.

Gideon's lips were light upon her own. A quick nip of his teeth on her bottom lip sent a streak of lightning all the way to her toes. Her hands gripped the edge of the table as emotions rushed through her—she wanted to grab him by the hair and force him closer, harder, more.

But Gideon's lips remained easy on her own, almost testing, as if he seemed to be waiting for her to push him away.

Right now, pushing him away was the last thing she had in mind.

Val felt his tongue teasing the seam of her lips and didn't even hesitate to let him in. When her tongue met his, fire exploded somewhere in the vicinity of where her stomach used to be. He kept it slow, kept it light and easy, until the fire threatened to consume her.

She was panting when he pulled away.

"Wow." It seemed to be the only thing she could say. Gideon had the same stunned expression on his face that she knew had to be on her own, and it made her happy. Guess she wasn't the only one the kiss had affected.

"Wow is right." His voice was deep and husky, with a smoky timbre to it that Val had never heard before.

She wanted to hear it again. Soon. Now. Right now.

And then she remembered that he was a Cupid, that he'd messed up her entire life, and the anger threatened to come back in full force.

"You didn't tell me the rest of it."

Gideon cleared his throat and shook his head as if to clear it. But Val had to give him credit. He didn't try to put off finishing the story. He laid it all out for her, from the time he'd found a match for her to the time the arrow had missed its mark and hit him instead.

He didn't even try to leave out the part that he was now in love with her, having suffered the effects of his own stray arrow.

Val wasn't quite sure how she felt about that. How could she now have a bond with a Cupid? It didn't seem feasible.

But that kiss. *Woah*. That kiss had rocked her, and if it was any indication of things to come, maybe being in love with a Cupid wouldn't be such a bad thing after all.

"So basically what you're telling me is that, since you shot yourself with the arrow that was intended for the man I'm supposed to live my life with, you've taken his place instead?"

"That's the condensed version, yes."

"I see." The thing was, she did see. Val could picture it all in her head, could see the way that it was going to work, whether she wanted it to happen this way or not. A large chain of events had been set into motion, all because of a gust of wind. But she'd asked for Cupid's help, and he'd definitely given it to her.

Not the way she'd expected, but beggars couldn't really be choosers, now could they?

"I need to think about this." She stood up, grabbing her coat and purse while trying not to fall over. Maybe tequila hadn't been a good idea after all.

"Let me get you a cab." Gideon's voice was still a little husky. He helped her into her coat, and she swore that she could feel the heat of his hand through the fabric at the small of her back.

"Thanks, but I think I'll just walk. It's only seven blocks."

She watched him look down at her and frown. "I think a cab might be safer. Or," he added, as her mouth opened in an instant rebuttal, "if you don't want a cab, at least let me walk you home. That way I can be sure you get there okay."

Val looked down at her hands, tightly clasped around her purse, and debated whether she should walk with him or not. It wasn't a bad idea, exactly, since she was feeling a little light-headed. What worried her was what would happen when they got to her apartment. She was still reeling from his kiss, and she still wanted him to kiss her again. That, along with the margaritas, could be a really bad combination.

But damn, she was destined to get closer to Gideon no matter which option she chose, wasn't she? Val figured she might as well get all of the pleasantries out of the way now, since she was already fated to get a whole lot more familiar with him in the near future.

"All right. You can walk me home, and we'll talk about how we're going to handle this whole mess on the way there. But no funny business. Cupid or not, destined to love or not, we'll do this the way any ordinary couple would do it. You understand?"

Gideon's smile was full of mischief and sexy as hell. "Yes, ma'am. I understand, and actually," he said, ushering her out the front door and onto the sidewalk, "I'm looking forward to it."

Six

The weekend was here, and for the first time in God knew how long, Val had a date.

Gideon had been a perfect gentleman the other night, when he walked her home from Trinity's. Part of her had hoped that he'd at least try to give her a good-night kiss at the door—even though she surely would have rebuffed him.

"Who am I kidding?" she mumbled to herself, searching around in her closet for something suitable to wear. "You know you wouldn't have turned him down. You wanted him to kiss you again. You *still* want him to kiss you again."

She had. She did.

Grabbing a sapphire blue dress that she knew brought out the color of her eyes, she laid it across the bed. Then sat down beside it.

For the past three days she'd done nothing but think of Gideon. Whatever he'd done, whatever type of spell he'd cast on her—on both of them—it was working. Even Mr. Allen's harping and blatant sexual innuendoes couldn't shake off her feeling that something great was going to happen.

Her workload grew larger as her productivity went down the toilet. She couldn't bring herself to be enthused over her customer's portfolios as she pondered the state of her love life. Even Tasha, when Val had finally given in and talked to her yesterday, wasn't able to shake Val's weird sense of having an out of body experience.

"Is this what it's like to go crazy?"

Since there was no one there to answer her, maybe she was going a little insane. The Cupid deal was beginning to work out a whole hell of a lot better than she'd planned, and she wasn't sure she was ready for it.

Val thought she'd been in love before. Years ago, there had been a man who she'd thought would be the one she'd spend the rest of her life with. But even Adam hadn't given her these weird feelings, these vibes, that she felt spinning throughout her body even when Gideon wasn't around.

Was this what being in love really felt like?

"Well, there's only one way to find out." She took special care to look good. Gideon was coming over for dinner, an invitation that she had spontaneously, and without warning, issued the other night when he'd walked her home. Bummed that he hadn't even tried for that good-night kiss, she'd blurted out that she would like to fix him dinner Saturday night.

He'd looked surprised, then amazed, as he'd answered that he'd love to come for dinner. With another sexy grin and a light touch of his hand upon her cheek, he'd walked away, leaving her feeling slightly tipsy and aroused outside her apartment building.

Now it was Saturday, dinner was warming in the oven, and she was trying to make herself look desirable yet not too eager for her date with Gideon.

She wanted to have sex with a Cupid. God, that sounded kinky. Yet just the thought of kissing him again, of having his hands and that wicked mouth on her, anywhere on her, had her heart rate speeding up and little shivers of desire working their way up and down her spine.

This surely had to be a sorry state of affairs.

If it was the last thing he did, he was going to kiss her again.

Gideon stood outside Val's door, a bouquet of yellow roses in one hand and the other hand poised to knock.

He'd given in and talked to McCabe about the whole thing. Finally going to work had actually eased some of the tension he'd been suffering from and, as unlikely as it sounded, McCabe had improved his mood even more.

"Go for it." His advice had been short and to the point, but he'd given Gideon the go-ahead to do what he'd wanted to do all along.

Now here he was, ready to have dinner with the woman that he was in love with. If he could just get through the meal without acting like an idiot, or suggesting that they go to bed like he really wanted them to do, all would be fine. He hoped.

He knocked once, and when almost a minute went by with no response, he raised his hand to knock again. Before he could connect with the door, it flew open in a whirlwind of motion—all he saw was long black hair flying, a short blue dress swirling, and spots that suddenly danced behind his eyes. And, of course, he felt quite well the rush of blood that landed somewhere below the waistband of his slacks.

"Hi." It was pretty lame as greetings went, but Gideon couldn't quite think straight. Val was gorgeous; he'd already known that, but tonight she was absolutely beautiful.

It wasn't helping to tamp down his love and desire to get her horizontal one bit.

"Hi. Are those for me?" She was looking at the flowers, and Gideon was looking at the smooth skin of her thigh he could see where the hem of her dress ended.

He cleared his throat and extended the roses to her, pulling up what he hoped would be a charming smile. "Yes. I heard a rumor that you were partial to yellow roses."

"Well, then, the rumor was right. Come in?"

Val backed up a step, and he made his way in. And then he stopped, only a hairbreadth and a bouquet of flowers separating their bodies in the doorway.

Looking down at her, thoughts swirled in his mind of what their future held, of what living with her for eternity would be like. Of what their children would look like. He thought of introducing her to his parents, and it warmed his heart. He thought, all in the space of less than a minute, of what living and loving with Valentine Lewis would be like.

It made the band of stress that had been circling his gut let go, and it left a feeling like none he'd ever known circulating throughout his body. Gideon loved Val, and if the look in her cerulean blue eyes as she stared up into his own was any indication, she felt the same way.

He was going to kiss her now, and to hell with the consequences. These were unusual circumstances, and he was an unusual guy. Val was, by all accounts, the most unusual woman he'd ever met. In his book, that called for desperate measures.

Gideon didn't ask for permission, or even wait to see if she would grant it. He wrapped one hand in that long silk curtain of dark hair, planted his other hand at her waist, and lowered his lips to hers as her mouth opened in surprise.

This was no casual kiss, no consoling touch of lips like the one he'd given her in the bar the other night. This was passion, flowing out of him and into her, and to his relief, vice versa.

Closer. He needed to get closer. It was the only thing he could think as her tongue touched his, as her hands lost their grip on the roses and he felt them instead in his hair.

He'd never tasted anything sweeter than her kiss.

Somewhere in the back of his mind, he heard sounds that were half-moans and half-pants, and he couldn't tell if they were coming from him or Val.

Gideon didn't really care. He left her lips long enough to trail his mouth over her cheek and lightly nipped her ear-lobe. Fighting the fire that was raging inside of him, he tried to slow down the burn that was surely going to ignite into a wildfire. He trailed his lips across her eyelids, down the bridge of her nose, down to her neck where he lightly licked the pulse that was beating there.

Val's hands were everywhere—in his hair, gripping his shoulders, at his waist. Letting his own hands wander, he ran them down the bare expanse of her arms and felt the flesh rise with goose bumps. Bringing his mouth back to hers, he lightly ran his palms down the silk of her dress at her waist, until his fingers lingered where the skirt ended.

She was a wiggling mass of desire pressed firmly against him, and Gideon suddenly felt like a virgin alone for the first time in the company of a ready and willing woman.

His mood was abruptly shattered when he realized that he *was* a virgin alone with a ready and willing woman for the first time.

Gideon forced himself to pull back gently, and the glazed look in her eyes had his erection growing larger and harder. Damn, but he hurt. He wanted to make love with Val, but he was suddenly confused and not a little afraid. This was the woman he was destined to love forever, and he needed to do this right. A quickie against her open apartment door wasn't what he'd had in mind.

He cleared his throat and ran his hand once more across the ebony silk of her hair. "Maybe we should shut the door, Val. And then we can talk about where this is leading."

Where this was leading? She knew damn well where it was leading. To her bed, if she had anything to say about it. Or the couch. Or damn it, they could just keep going right where they were standing. Oh dear God, what was she thinking? Was she crazy?

But Gideon looked so good, hair rumpled and eyes wide with desire. And she could feel him, still, the way his erection had pushed against her belly and caused a fire to light there.

It had been a very long time since Val had felt that rush of passion. When she mixed in the love that was churning around her heart, it was one heck of a heady feeling. And now the nitwit wanted to talk—again. Maybe that was good. Maybe it would calm her beating heart, would give her time to figure out what she felt, what she wanted. Give her time to contemplate what being in love—and lust—with a Cupid really meant.

She took a deep breath and picked up her roses from where they'd fallen on the floor. Turning away from him, she left Gideon to close the door. She had to smile when she heard the locks, all three of them, slide closed.

"Would you like something to drink? I'll have dinner on the table in about fifteen minutes."

Val glanced back over her shoulder as she opened the refrigerator and noticed that Gideon hadn't moved from his spot just inside the doorway.

"You can come in," she laughed.

He finally moved, hesitantly it seemed, to perch on the edge of her cream-colored sofa. Val poured them each a glass of wine, then picked up her roses from the counter. Rummaging around under her kitchen cabinets, she finally found a cut-glass vase. Filling the vase with water, adding just a pinch of sugar the way her mother had taught her, then adding the flowers gave her something to do with her hands.

When she'd finally placed the vase in the middle of her small table, she had nothing left to do but take Gideon his wine. Suddenly, she was nervous, and the only way to get rid of it was to keep busy—keep talking.

She sat on the matching chair across from him, a glass

and bronze coffee table between them. Handing him his glass, she smiled into his eyes, and felt a shiver run through her at the desire she saw there.

Seems he hadn't been as unaffected by their kiss as she'd thought.

"Well then. What should we talk about?"

"Anything you'd like."

Not much of a talker tonight, but that was okay, since no one had ever called her shy and quiet.

"How old are you?" It was a question that had been burning a hole in her head for days.

Gideon's eyes widened slightly and Val watched as he took a gulp of wine. "Yes, well, I guess you got right to the point, didn't you?"

"Is that a problem?"

"No." He looked down into his wineglass, fingering the stem nervously. "I just don't want you to panic when I tell you."

Val's laughter sounded slightly hysterical, even to her own ears. "Why in God's name would I panic? You can't be, what, more than thirty-five or so."

"Thirty-two."

"Well, then, see, that wasn't so bad, now was it?"

"One hundred and thirty-two."

The wine she'd just swallowed got stuck somewhere on its way down. She didn't choke, but it was close. It landed, at last, with a thud in the pit of her stomach, and her hand clenched the glass so hard she was afraid it might shatter. *Holy hell, please tell me he didn't just say what I know he just said.*

"Tell me I heard you wrong."

Gideon finally glanced up from the liquid in his glass and smiled. It looked a little ragged at the edges, but he was trying. "You didn't hear me wrong."

"I was afraid you were going to say that." Val sat her wine down on the coffee table and quickly rose. "Let me get dinner out of the oven, and then we'll talk about this some more." *After I have time to figure out what I'm supposed to do with a man, a Cupid, who is over one hundred years old. What the hell is happening to me?*

As she removed the roast from the oven, it occurred to her that they'd been doing a lot of talking lately. Seems that all they did, really, was talk—and yet she still had so many questions that it felt as if her head would explode with them.

Would it ever end? Would she ever know everything there was to know in this situation?

As she set out serving dishes and placed the rolls in a basket, she realized that it might not even matter. Did two people ever know everything about each other? All couples had secrets, or if not secrets, had things about themselves, about their pasts, that didn't come up until later in their relationship. Was this any different?

Sure, she wanted to know how being a Cupid worked. She wanted to know how he spent his days, and his nights. Val wanted to know about his family, his ethics, the things that made him sad and those that made him happy.

And she wanted to know what he looked like naked.

Her hands shook so badly on that last thought that the basket she'd been holding hit the tabletop with a bang, and rolls spilled over the top to land next to her vase. Naked. Well. That about summed it up, didn't it?

"It's time to eat."

They sat across from each other, a quiet settling between them that wasn't all that pleasant. Here she was, Miss Can't-shut-me-up-if-you-slapped-duct-tape-over-my-mouth, and she couldn't think of a thing to say to the man sitting across from her.

Val cleaned her plate in silence. She could hear the ticking of her kitchen clock, which sounded ungodly loud this evening. She even swore that the sounds of her chewing were echoing off canyons somewhere. Dear God, had she ever gone this long without talking?

It was too much. Here she was, sitting across from a man who she undeniably had feelings for, and they were studiously avoiding contact. They weren't even looking at each other, for Pete's sake. The craziness had gone on long enough. Valentine was a woman of action, by God, and if ever there was a time for action, this was it. Manners be damned, because it was show time.

"Enough." It had come out louder than she'd intended, and Gideon's fork dropping onto his plate sounded like a ricocheting bullet in her small kitchen area. "What the hell are we doing, Gideon?"

He cleared his throat, but he at least looked at her. That was an improvement. "I think we're trying to get comfortable with each other, and it doesn't seem to be working."

"You can say that again. Okay, enough of this crap." Val pushed her chair back from the table and placed her hands, palms down, on the table. Leaning toward him, she saw his eyes widen and a smile tug at the corners of his lips.

Her face was only inches from his, and she could see her reflection in the velvety smoothness of his brown eyes. Val had never been so intrigued with a man's eyes before—then again, she'd never felt like she was free-falling into a lake with no bottom.

"I think we need to cut to the chase, as they say. You're a Cupid, I'm not. You're over a hundred years old, and I'm not. Those are the obvious." She took a deep breath and leaned closer still, until her lips were only a breath away from Gideon's. "What's not so obvious, at least on the outside, is the fact that we're in the middle of something that neither of us can stop. I have feelings for you that I've never felt for anyone else. I can't say it's love, not yet, because I'm just not sure. But there's something there, and a lot of it is chemistry."

Val leaned forward, until her mouth was at the corner of his lips. "I'm thinking that the chemistry between us is just about hot enough to self-combust. And I really, really want to find out if that's true." She flicked her tongue out, just enough to wet his bottom lip, and something unfurled deep in her belly at his hiss of indrawn breath.

"So why don't we leave the niceties to later, and work on the chemistry first. Come to bed with me, Gideon, and show me what a Cupid can do."

Seven

January 20, 2004
Cupid Headquarters
Circle of the Three

"Should we intervene, Your Excellence?" Dimitria's voice was soft, a tinkling of chimes on a windy day. "I don't know if we should allow Gideon to, well . . ." Her words died off as her hands fluttered before her.

Eros let out a chuckle, raising an eyebrow at Dimitria's stern look of disapproval. The look on Jonathan's face was one he didn't think he'd ever forget. Gideon's father was hovering somewhere between disbelief and horror, and Eros had to admit that it was quite humorous to watch.

"We have let this thing go on this long without intervention. Why should I stir the pot with my own hand now?"

"Eros," Dimitria said, "you know why. Gideon is about to . . . he's thinking about . . . I think he's going to . . ." Her words ended on a sigh of frustration. "You know what I'm talking about."

His laugh was deep and bounced off the chamber where the Circle had convened. "Of course, dear lady, I know what you're talking about. Is it the right choice, this path that Gideon and Valentine Lewis are embarking on? I cannot say for sure. But I will tell you one thing, both of you."

He moved around on his throne, turning to face his consorts. "I will not interfere with what the gods have begun. I have learned, in all of these thousands of years, that things happen for a reason. Your son, Jonathan, was destined to be Val's soul mate. Can I explain it? Of course not. But I know it to be true, and I will not interfere.

"So my dear, dear Dimitria, we will close the curtains now and let Gideon follow his own path. I think that this is one job that our boy can figure out all on his own."

January 20, 2004
Val's Bedroom

Gideon was trapped in a purgatory of his own making. Hovering in some nowhere land between sheer terror and absolute delight at knowing that he was going to have sex with Val, he had no idea what to do.

How the hell did you tell the woman you loved that you were a one-hundred-thirty-two-year-old virgin?

Gee, Val, the thing is, I love you with all of my heart and soul, but there's something you need to know. When I take my clothes off, you're going to see my wings—and oh, by the way, I've never had sex before.

Yeah. That was going to go over real well.

So instead of thinking, he let his mind wander over nothing as Val led him down the hallway and into the bedroom. Once there, in the darkness that was only slightly alleviated by a sliver of moon shining through her window, she turned to him, her body fitting perfectly with his.

Now this he could do. All he had to do was give in to the passion that flowed through his veins, the need and desire to be with this woman, and he could act with confidence.

Gideon felt Val's arms on his back. It seemed that his every nerve ending was attuned to her—to the way she smelled, like tropical flowers after a rain. To the way she felt, soft and pliant against his own hard body. Even the way she moved her palms in slow circles against his back. He could feel her breath through the material of his shirt.

He brought one hand up to smooth the hair back from her face, then let it linger, along her cheek, down the fine arch of her neck, across one shoulder as he made his way down to her waist. His thumb brushed, ever so lightly, against the outer curve of her breast on his way down. Gideon heard her breath stumble, felt her hands grab his shirt as she moved closer to him.

It seemed to be as elemental, as timeless, as time itself. He might not know the intricacies of making love, but he knew, deep down inside where it mattered, that he could please her. Small touches, light caresses upon her body, would bring her to a pinnacle of desire that he alone would be able to take her over.

The thought thrilled him. It didn't matter that he was inexperienced. What mattered was that right now, at this perfect moment in time, they were together, edging toward something that neither one of them was likely to forget.

The body, it seemed, didn't need a guide to do what it was created to do. As Gideon brought his body into even closer alignment with Val's, as his head lowered to press his lips to her own, he gave into the truth that he'd somehow known all along.

Love speaks its own language.

Val wanted to gobble him up in one quick bite. It had been so long, probably too long, since she'd been held by a man who cared about her. Actually, this was a new experience for her, in that she knew that Gideon not only cared, he loved her. It was a heady feeling, to be loved and desired by a man. And to have that desire racing through her own body only added to her pleasure. Add to that the feelings that she had for him, and it was a very potent combination.

Did she love him? As his lips touched her own, as she felt her mouth open at the prodding of his tongue, she felt that she must. Her hands trembled on his back as she pushed herself closer into him—striving, reaching, straining toward something, anything.

Gideon's tongue invaded her mouth, plundered and took and took until her breath was gone and her legs felt like half-set Jell-O. Val rubbed herself shamelessly against him, needing the feel of him, all of him, against her.

"We're wearing too many damn clothes." She didn't realize she'd spoken the words against his lips until she felt his hands on the back of her thighs grab her tighter and felt his dick jump against her belly.

She'd deliberately worn the short blue dress to entice him. It seemed to be working, as his hands, those oh-so-talented hands, were everywhere. Val felt his light caresses on the backs of her thighs, felt the smooth hardness of his palms as they rode higher, toward her ass. Their mouths were still dueling, both fighting to give and take.

Feeling a slight stir of air, she opened her eyes to see that he'd reversed their positions. He was now sitting on the side of her queen-size bed, and she was standing in the open circle of his legs. Val couldn't help but notice that her breasts were level with his mouth.

"Take off your dress." It was uttered in a deep voice, rough at the edges. For a moment she hesitated, but it didn't last long. After all, it had been her idea to take him to bed, and she wouldn't chicken out now.

Val reached behind to undo the button that held the material closed against the back of her neck. Suddenly embarrassed, she glanced down as the dress fell, over her breasts, past her hips, to lie in a puddle at her feet. Gideon's hands grasped her waist as she straightened up.

She'd worn the dress for him, but the ice-blue scraps of lace that covered her full breasts and the mound of her womanhood had been all for her. Val never felt sexier than when she wore sexy underwear. She'd never expected Gideon to see it. Or had she? Hadn't she known, somewhere in the back of her mind, that this night would end up here?

Desire had rooted permanently in her belly since she'd first seen him. Sure, it had warred with the anger and embarrassment of his mistake, but the lust had always been there. So surely she'd known, when dressing for their dinner date tonight, that the scraps that covered her were for his enjoyment as much as her own.

She was thrown from her moment of self-discovery by the feel of something warm and wet just above her belly button. Val glanced down, and when she saw the top of Gideon's mane of blond hair, and caught a peek of his tongue tracing a path of hot, wet fire along her belly, the tremors that had recently left her legs came back with a vengeance.

Along with a reciprocating wetness between her thighs.

She was going to come undone before they even had a chance to get started. But she knew then that this wasn't simply a case of having gone too long without the touch of a man. This was something bigger, something better, than mere attraction. And then it came to her, swiftly, the knowledge that she'd had all along.

"I love you, Gideon." His mouth stilled its foray on her abdomen, and he glanced up into her eyes. A smile lit up his entire face, and for the first time, he looked like the almost cherubic man that Val already knew he was.

"I know. And I love you, Valentine, with all of my heart."

What else was there to say after that? Val let herself be taken over by the feelings that were churning in her body.

She closed her eyes and her head fell back as she felt his hands, so gentle, upon her breasts. As his thumbs flicked over the sensitive buds of her nipples, a moan escaped her throat. As if following some internal cue that she'd given him, his thumbs flicked them again, harder this time. Over and over, until her nipples were so sensitive that she felt every pull, every stroke, in her very core.

And then his mouth was there, on those swollen nubs, licking her through the lace that was no barrier at all. He clasped her gently with his teeth, and his first tug upon one crest had her hands grabbing the back of his head and urging him closer.

As he suckled one breast, then the other, she felt his fingers dance their way to her waist, down to her hips, to the crease where the lace ended and her skin began. Light touches upon the inside of her thighs had her legs trembling, her back arching, and her hands reaching to touch him.

"Take off your shirt, Gideon, please. I want to feel your skin against mine."

When he pulled away to do as she'd asked, she felt almost lost. She wanted contact, wanted to rub herself against him like a cat. And then he was there, shirtless, and Val's hands roamed aimlessly over the firm, hard muscles of his chest. She looked down, and in the moonlight, saw a light sprinkling of hair across his pectoral muscles, angling sharply down into a narrow patch that disappeared beneath the waistband of his pants.

"The pants, too, Gideon."

His smile was bright and full of love as he stood before her. When he was left only in a pair of silk boxers, she brought herself full up against him. That first contact left her breathless.

Suddenly their hands were everywhere. Val tried to reach everything, touch everything, as his mouth once again took hers. She didn't remember falling onto the bed, but she was there, straddling him, as Gideon's hands gripped her ass.

She was shameless. She rubbed herself against him, her smoothness against his erection that strained at the confines of silk holding him in. Val kissed him everywhere: his face, his shoulder, his chest. She let her tongue follow the path that the vee of hair made down his body. That wasn't enough, though, so she lowered herself until her mouth hovered over him under the silk. It was cool beneath her cheek.

Val leaned closer, inhaling his musky scent, and wrapped her lips around the head of his dick. Through the boxers she pulled him into the wet confines of her mouth, and delighted when his body arched off the bed like a bow.

"Val. Val." His voice didn't even sound like the one she'd become so accustomed to. His hands were on the back of her head, pulling her closer or pushing her away, she didn't know.

But then their positions were reversed, and her bra was pulled down with one rough hand. Then his mouth was there, devouring her, licking her, stirring her into a frenzy as she pushed her mound against the hard, throbbing flesh of his arousal.

And it still wasn't enough.

"Now, Gideon. Please, now." Val raised her hips and took off the lace panties herself. As she helped him out of the briefs, she caught one quick glimpse of blond curls surrounding the smooth, velvety steel of him. She wrapped her hand around it as she bit his earlobe, positioning him at her entrance.

Then she remembered that they weren't using protection. It almost stopped her cold, but her body wouldn't stop moving, and she couldn't stop rubbing her breasts against him.

"Gideon. Wait, Gideon." He was poised at her entrance, and Val wanted nothing more than to feel him coming inside of her in one quick thrust. "Gideon." When he opened his eyes, wide and glazed with desire that she knew was mirrored in her own, she said what needed to be said. "I don't have a condom, Gideon."

His brow furrowed, and for a moment he looked as if he had no idea what she was talking about. But then the smile was back, the one that warmed her from the inside out. "It's all right, luv, it's okay. I can't make babies until it's been sanctioned by Eros."

Val wasn't sure she'd heard him right. But she'd heard the "can't make babies" part loud and clear, even through the fog of desire that made her brain cloudy. They could talk about the rest later.

And then he was there, at the juncture between her thighs. A gasp escaped her lips as he slipped inside. A little more, a little farther, and he was embedded inside of her.

Val arched her hips, feeling him slide in a little deeper, and as his lips took possession of hers once again, he began to move.

It was slow and easy, an introduction of two bodies that were finding their own rhythm. But then that wasn't enough either, and she moved against him, raising her legs to wrap them around his waist.

"Dear God." She felt his hiss of breath against her lips and smiled, matching the motion of his thrusts.

Harder, faster, more. That's all she could think as his mouth once again descended on her breast, sucking a nipple deep into his mouth. Then she felt his hand at the nest of curls between her legs, prodding, stroking against her clit, and knew that she'd almost reached the top of her desire.

Gideon was pumping faster now, stroking her harder, and as her nails dug into the cheeks of his ass she heard herself cry out his name. Her climax overtook her, throwing her over a cliff that never seemed to end. She heard him breathing hard, felt the shivers that racked his body, and held on as he followed her over.

Val had come home.

If this was dying, he'd gladly stay dead forever. As Gideon lay beside Val, though, he realized he didn't want to be dead after all. If he were dead, he couldn't make love to her again, and he really, really wanted to make love to her again. Maybe in about ten minutes or so, if he had anything to say about it.

He was glad that his first time had been with the woman he would marry. He would tell her too, but later. Right now, all he wanted to do was lay like this, with Val's breasts against his back, her leg thrown over his own as the moonlight silvered the bed.

"I do love you, Gideon." Her voice was still husky, and it aroused him once again. Her hand made lazy circles over his thigh, then moved onto his back. He felt her fingers trace his backbone, then still as she felt the slight rise at his shoulder blade. Gideon felt rather than saw her raise herself up on one elbow, her fingers tracing across his back to his other shoulder, where an identical rise rested.

"What are these bumps?"

He might not tell her that this had just been his first time at having sex, but there was no way out of showing her his wings.

Gideon rolled away from her and stood beside the bed. My God, she looked so gorgeous, lying there with her black hair spread across the pillow, her skin almost glowing in the light from the moon.

Before he could talk himself out of it, he kept his eyes on her face and opened his wings. They were large, almost seven feet across when unfurled, a pearly, opalescent white with golden tips.

He watched her face carefully for signs of revulsion or anger. Instead, except for a widening of her eyes, she didn't show much emotion at all.

"You know," she said as a slight smile curved her lips, "I don't think anything you can do will surprise me anymore." Gideon watched as she came to her knees on the edge of the bed. "Can I touch them?"

He laughed. "You can touch anything you want, luv."

Her hands were light, tentative, as she slowly stroked one wing from the tip to where it met his shoulder.

"I love you, Gideon. Wings and all."

As he brought his mouth down to once again take hers in a kiss, he told himself to remember to thank McCabe. After all, without his "go for it" remark, he'd still be curled up into a ball in his own bed.

He also needed to thank the Circle of the Three, but as Val's tongue entered his mouth, warring with his own, and as his hands reached out to pull her closer, he decided that that could wait for another day.

Epilogue

February 13, 2004
Cupid Headquarters
Main Auditorium

He'd finally made it. As Eros presented him with his Cupid diploma, Gideon couldn't help but feel enormously happy, and relieved. His father smiled down at him from where the Circle of the Three sat upon their raised dais. His mother was in the audience, and he could see her wiping her tears with a white handkerchief. Then his gaze met Val's, and he knew that this moment, although he'd never forget it, paled in comparison to all of the moments he'd yet to spend with Val.

Gideon's life was finally complete. He was no longer a winger, no longer just a Cupid-in-training, no longer alone. He had a woman whom he loved more than life itself. His family had welcomed her with open arms, and in just a few weeks, Gideon would meet Val's family. He had a career, his own home, a loving family, and the most gorgeous wife-to-be.

McCabe was jealous. It made Gideon grin to think of it. Poor guy now wanted someone of his own.

As he made his way back to the line of graduating Cupids, his heart was full.

February 13, 2004
Eros' Private Chambers

Eros was once again in his favorite chair before the fire, drink beside him on the table, Agape lounging on the footstool in front of him. It had been a busy day, and an even more eventful two months.

Agape's meow was loud, startling Eros from his reverie. As his thoughts entered his own mind, he scoffed.

"Don't be absurd, dear friend. I knew all along that everything would work out."

As the cat's meow came again, sounding sarcastically like a rebuttal, Eros smiled. "All right, all right. I may have had my doubts in the beginning about Gideon's ability to handle the situation, but it all worked out just fine, now didn't it?"

He raised his glass and took a swallow, and as the fire burned in the hearth and the liquid warmed his belly, he smiled at his companion. "I wonder what mystery is in store for us next?"

As the cat's thoughts washed over him, he chuckled yet again. Maybe his friend Agape was right. Maybe things would settle back down into the quiet, smooth order that they'd always been. Then again, a little upheaval every now and then never hurt anyone. Plus, he had a feeling that since Gideon had changed the rules on them all, even unknowingly, there were going to be plenty of things in the future to keep him busy.

February 14, 2004
Val's Journal

Well here it is, my twenty-eighth birthday, and it seems that I knew what I was doing all along. I suppose, though, that I can't claim all the credit. My sister thought I was crazy to rely on a Cupid to find me a mate. Hell, even I thought I was crazy a time or two in the last few weeks. But as the old cliché goes, "all's well that ends well."

I'm guessing that over the next five hundred years or so, I'll learn all there is to know about Gideon. As of now, in the beginning of our relationship, we're still in that new stage. Still getting to know each other, still learning about the things that make us tick. Still, thank God, learning each other's bodies. I readily admit, as the still mortal woman that I am, that the exploring bodies part is still my favorite.

His family is wonderful. McCabe is, well, McCabe. He actually reminds me a lot of my sister, but don't tell her I said that. So far, the one time they've met, they avoided each other like the plague.

Gideon told me yesterday that he'd been a virgin the first time we made love. I think my total exclamation of surprise, along with my comment that I'd never have known, made him happy. I guess no one, Cupid or not, wants to think that they blew their first time.

On another note, Mr. Allen has given me a promotion. Although he's still an idiot, and still perverted, he's finally recognized my supreme talent in the accounting department. Valentine Lewis, Assistant Manager. It has a nice ring to it.

I've been wondering lately exactly what would have happened to me, and to Gideon, if he hadn't shot himself with that arrow. Would the man he'd chosen for me be as perfectly compatible as Gideon himself is? I've decided not to think about it too much, over-analyze it, as it's bound to drive me crazy.

But that leads me to another thought. Exactly where did Gideon hit himself with the arrow? I'll ask him, tonight after the dinner and movie we're planning on attending. Maybe I'll even wait until after the after, if you get my drift.

Love, with all its ups, downs, and in-betweens, is turning out to be a wonderful thing. I have a Cupid to thank for that.

December 24, 2004
Gideon and Val's Home

They'd decided to hold a Christmas Eve party at their home. The wedding had been a month earlier, a glorious affair that although simple and elegant, had been Val's dream come true.

Now it was just family—her family, including Tasha, her mother and her father, Gideon's parents, and McCabe. Seems McCabe had no plans for Christmas, and Val wouldn't let him sit at home alone during the holidays.

As she stood with Tasha near the bar, she watched her sister shoot daggers toward where the rest of the family was gathered in the dining room. For some reason, Tasha and McCabe had been circling each other like fighting dogs since they'd been introduced months ago. Val couldn't get a handle on it.

"What's with you tonight? If looks could kill, and if McCabe could actually *be* killed, he'd be a dead man."

Tasha turned toward her sister, eggnog in hand. "He irritates the hell out of me."

Val frowned. "How in the world could he irritate you? You've only met him once before. You usually have more tolerance than that."

At her sister's quick blush, Val's eyes widened. "What are you not telling me?"

"Nothing." But it was said too quickly, and Val was much too persistent to let it go at that.

"Spill it, sis. I mean it. What's up with you and McCabe?"

Tasha looked around, making sure no one else was in earshot. Val's sister was the only one of her family and friends who knew what Gideon really was. She and Gideon had decided not to alarm her parents—or force them into an early grave—by announcing the fact that he was a Cupid. The arrangement, so far, was working out well.

Her sister took a deep breath and leaned toward her. "He's irritating. He's a damn macho Cupid, a throwback to the days when men didn't believe women could think for themselves. His perfect idea of a wife is a little lady who will tell him how great he is and make sure dinner is on the table at six. God, I just want to throttle him."

She pushed her hair back in frustration, then took another long drink from her glass. "But that's not even the worse part. Oh no. Have you looked at him, Val? He's sexy as hell. That *so* pisses me off."

Val stared at her sister in amazement. "You've got the hots for him."

"I do not." The outrage sounded false, even to Tasha's own ears. "I just . . . okay, fine, I've got the hots for him. But I can live with that. What really irks me is that he seems to have the hots for me too, and he won't leave me the hell alone."

Val smiled at her sister. "Just tell him you're not interested."

"I can't. Damn it, I can't."

"And you can't because?" She left it hanging as a question, waiting for her sister to admit that she was just as attracted to McCabe as he was to her.

"Shit, Val, I can't leave him alone. I already made a big mistake, and it's too late to fix it."

"What in the world are you talking about?"

Tasha looked down at the floor, then glared over at McCabe, who was grinning at them for all the world like a cat who had just caught a huge, juicy mouse for his master. "Because in a moment of drunken loneliness, I asked for McCabe for Christmas, and it seems like I got him."

Val's jaw dropped, and then she laughed so hard that tears rolled down her cheeks. As everyone in the other room stopped talking and turned to stare at her, she laughed and laughed until she had to double over and hold her stomach.

Her sister. And McCabe. Another Cupid in the family. God, she wanted to be a fly on the wall when Tasha got her claws into him.

MESMERIZED

Jordan Summers

One

Cluck, cluck, cluck. Quack, quack, quack. Oink, oink, oink. Hee-haw, hee-haw, hee-haw.

Amanda Dillon's eyes widened and her head snapped around as the last hee-haw faded. She glanced at the five gorgeous men crawling around at her feet like barnyard animals, each one more delicious-looking than the last.

Someone was certainly getting into it tonight.

A smile played at the corners of her mouth as she snapped her fingers twice. "Woo me!" she shouted. "Win me over with your professions of love." The men instantly transformed from helpless critters to wanna-be Romeos all vying for her attention.

If only it were that easy in real life.

One recited poetry, while another blond Adonis crouched on bended knee, attempting to sing a love ballad. It was a good thing he was gorgeous, because cats fighting in a garbage can maintained better pitch. Amanda turned from the crooner long enough to look at the audience, which consisted mainly of women, who broke into giggles at the sight before them.

Amanda pinched her nose and waved her hand in front of her face. The crowd roared. She'd earned the reputation as the "Man Tamer of Manhattan" after two years of sold out shows. Amanda looked around the small hardwood floor stage half expecting to see a stool and a whip appear.

"Man Tamer of Manhattan." She snorted under her breath. If they only knew the truth.

She wasn't particularly proud of the nickname, but it did pay the bills—and kept men at bay. A rather disappointing repercussion of achieving success that, willing or not, she'd grown accustomed to. Not that she had the time or inclination to date. Her jaundiced gaze scanned the men. These same types of men validated her career-imposed celibacy every night.

Amanda smiled wistfully, and then turned back to the Lotharios. The men groveled and begged as she rolled her eyes. Every woman's fantasy. *Hardly.*

Each performance was the same. Amanda was bored with the act and it showed. If only she could find something to liven it up. Then again, was it her act—or her life that needed livening as of late? Amanda wasn't sure and decided not to delve too deeply into her thoughts.

Heck, she'd settle for finding a man who would be into a no-strings kind of relationship, who didn't require induction in order to tell the truth.

Come back to planet Earth, Amanda. It isn't going to happen.

One bold man on stage took that moment to snatch her hand in his, shaking Amanda from her thoughts. Not you, sweetheart, she mused, as the man began placing Gomez-style kisses along the length of her arm. Amanda chortled and fought to keep from laughing louder, before extracting her hand.

Ah, well . . . time for the big finale.

She pasted a smile on her face and raised her arms. "When I count to five you will awake feeling refreshed and rested, as if you've had an hour-long nap filled with pleasurable dreams. One, two, you're feeling more awake and aware of your surroundings, three, four, sounds in the room are growing louder, five, open your eyes." Amanda snapped her fingers twice.

The men blinked, looking around, brows knitted in confusion. They took in their surroundings as if for the first time. One particularly cocky participant stood, stretching his limbs before resting his massive arms across his wide muscular chest.

At another time in her life, Amanda would've found the man attractive and desirable, but not now. To her jaded eyes, he looked like a Neanderthal ready to beat his chest for attention. *No thanks.*

"See, I told you I couldn't be hypnotized," he said, his head bobbing, as a mocking grin spread over his chiseled face.

As tempting as it was to knock the smile from his mouth, Amanda didn't have to.

The audience burst out laughing at his bravado as Amanda went to the side of the stage and retrieved the complimentary videotape the men received for their participation.

She smiled at the man who'd made the outburst, this time for real, as she handed him his copy. His cheeks flushed red and his eyes flashed, promising her retribution.

Amanda had seen it all before. A week from now he'd laugh about the whole event. "Enjoy the show," she said, winking at him, a moment before she turned to the audience to bid them good night.

The crowd came to their feet in a standing ovation. Amanda bowed deep, and then rose. "How about a round of applause for our good sports?" She waved a hand in the direction of the men, who were brushing their pants off and straightening their clothes.

The applause and wolf whistles grew louder. A stagehand gathered the participants together, and then led them back to their seats. Amanda bowed one last time, before exiting stage right.

Someone handed her a towel as she made her way down a long corridor to her dressing room. She dabbed at the moisture on her face.

The tiny dressing room held a small navy blue couch with worn cushions, a black coffee table big enough to place refreshments on, a changing screen, and a lighted vanity with a white wicker chair shoved in front of it. Nothing fancy, but it was hers.

Amanda stepped inside and closed the door behind her. She rested her back against the hard wood for a couple of breaths and then pushed away. The room was filled to the brim with floral baskets and bouquets. The blooms' sweet scents reached her nose. Amanda's eyes watered and her throat began to itch.

"Perfect," she groaned.

The tediousness of tonight's show weighed heavily on her shoulders. The audience deserved better than her split attention.

The show's success had reached beyond her wildest dreams. She'd hoped to have a couple months' run, but the popularity of the performance guaranteed bookings through the end of the year. It also guaranteed a new kind of pressure, one that required her to expand the show or eventually go bust. Unfortunately, the only way to do that was to promote in the media. She shuddered at the thought.

Amanda received calls daily from every major network and magazine, begging her to grant them an interview or, as she liked to think of it, a chance to rip her "Man Tamer of Manhattan" persona to shreds.

Amanda sighed as she plopped into the wicker chair and began removing her stage makeup, which was thick enough to require a spatula.

She stared at her reflection, before exhaling loudly. She looked tired, weak, stretched thin from so many performances. Her normally sparkling eyes looked wary.

When had that happened? When had the flicker of excitement and rush from performing left her? Had she always been so cynical? A resounding "yes" clamored in her head. Amanda rolled her eyes.

The press could detect weakness at a thousand clicks, which left Amanda stuck between a rock and a smashed place.

The magazines and networks might as well pack it in, because she couldn't afford to give any of them an opportunity to tear down what she'd created.

Amanda had removed all but two remaining spots of makeup when a knock sounded at the door. "Who is it?" she asked, ears straining for a voice.

She'd learned the hard way not to grant entry without first identifying the caller. The last time that occurred Amanda had found herself eye to belt buckle with one of her audience participants. He'd signed a release like every other participant in the show, but from the crumpled piece of paper in his fist, Amanda deduced he didn't care.

Luckily, her assistant Wendy had arrived and removed the man with a little finesse. Amanda smiled. Wendy was worth every penny Amanda paid her and then some. The knock sounded again with more force.

"Who is it?"

"It's me, Wendy." Her assistant's voice rose.

Speak of the she-devil. "Come in."

Wendy bounced into the room like a ray of sunshine on speed, her russet-colored ponytail swishing from side to side, as she dropped onto the couch. Wearing a pair of designer striped pants with a pullover sweater, the hip clothing fit her lithe form perfectly. Known for her upbeat personality, Wendy filled any space she entered with her larger than life optimism. At parties, everyone gravitated toward her like planets to the sun, drawn by her warmth.

Amanda was exactly opposite to the woman she called friend and assistant. In the solar system of life, she'd be Pluto. Where Wendy exuded warmth, Amanda cultivated the ability to give any man frostbite if he stood too close.

Originally meant to keep her focused on building her career, aloofness wasn't something she could control any longer. It just occurred and felt comfortable, like shrugging on a well-worn coat.

Amanda was well aware of her ice queen reputation,

which was why she'd hired Wendy. The perfect buffer to an otherwise unfriendly world.

"How was it tonight?" Wendy asked, tugging at her lower lip with her teeth.

"Same ol', same ol'," Amanda answered, staring at Wendy from the mirror. She froze as her assistant's expression permeated her thoughts. Amanda turned. "What's up?"

Wendy fidgeted. "I don't know what you mean."

"Wendy Ann . . ." She only used Wendy's middle name when she knew her friend was lying. "You never bite your lip unless you have bad news to tell me or you know I'm not going to like what you have to say."

The normally cheerful woman grimaced. "I guess I should work on schooling my face."

Amanda laughed. "Not a chance. I like being able to read exactly what you're thinking. You've got a face poker players dream of competing against."

Wendy giggled.

"Now tell me what's up."

"Do you like the flowers?"

Atch-oo. "Yes, they're lovely. Now quit stalling."

Her assistant shrugged, drawing her feet under her legs. "You received another message, along with all these flowers from that journalist at *Mode Times Magazine.*"

"What's his name again?" Amanda sniffled.

Wendy stilled, her brow furrowing as she concentrated. "You know, I never caught it."

"That's weird. Normally star journalists love the sound of their names rolling off their lips." Amanda frowned. "How many messages does that make?"

"Fifteen, not counting today's note."

"Did he send *all* these flowers?"

"Yep."

"He's persistent, I'll give him that." Amanda sneezed, and then wiped the last two smudges of makeup away. "Is that all?"

Wendy shifted again under her scrutiny. "I was just thinking maybe you should grant him an interview."

Amanda's eyes widened. "Why would I want to do that? Do you think he's found a way into my heart through my hay fever?"

Wendy bit her lip to keep from laughing, and then pretended to pluck fuzz from her sweater. "No, I think you should do it because he sounds kind of sexy and he's always polite."

"Sounds sexy, eh?" Amanda arched a brow and began applying moisturizer. "You aren't trying to play matchmaker again, are you?"

"Yes to the first question and no to the second." Wendy bit her lip once more.

Amanda's stomach tightened. Her friend had fibbed again. She tilted her head to get a better look at Wendy in the mirror. Amanda didn't know what her assistant was up to but she didn't like it. She paused, her gaze locked on her friend, and then she carefully phrased her question. "When did you last speak with him?"

"Yesterday, when he phoned."

Amanda spun around to face Wendy, her heart slamming into her ribs. "You didn't tell him I'd grant an interview, did you? Don't you remember what happened to my father? One stupid article by one reporter and his life was ruined. Do you want that to happen to me?" Her eyes searched her friend's face as panic set in. Oh God, the last thing she needed was some strange man showing up at her door.

Wendy waved a hand in the air. "Calm down. Of course not. I'd never do anything like that without your permission. I know your reasons for not granting interviews. And you know I'm sorry about your dad. I just thought that maybe it was time to reconsider. This is your career, not his."

"I don't think so." Amanda humphed. "Every time I consider changing my mind, I picture my father working himself to death, trying to rebuild a reputation that one article shattered beyond repair," she stated firmly, before her gaze narrowed in suspicion. "If you didn't agree to an interview, then what did you say?"

Wendy shrugged, but the action didn't look nonchalant. "I told him to stop by the show and ask you himself."

Amanda felt the air squeeze from her lungs. It was one thing to turn someone down via e-mail or phone, it was quite another to look them in the face while doing so. "You didn't," she murmured in disbelief.

Wendy grinned sheepishly. "I did."

"Why? You're supposed to be my defense against the dark side."

Her friend giggled. "I am, *Luke*, but what's it going to hurt? He may look as good as he sounds," she said, waggling her eyebrows.

"I doubt it." Amanda soured, dropping her head in her hands. "Oh Wendy, what have you done?" she asked, peeking through two fingers.

"Nothing that isn't good for you." Her friend bounced up from the couch and sashayed to the door. She glanced over her shoulder one last time. "There is such a thing as dating and sex in the world, remember? Besides, if you don't want him, I'll take him." Wendy winked, and then exited.

Amanda groaned. She didn't need a journalist for anything, not even a sexy sounding one. Wendy could have him with her blessing.

Note to self: kill smart-mouthed assistant.

Derek Armstrong sat in his office, smiling to himself. He'd finally managed to get a foot in the door of the "Man Tamer of Manhattan." An impossible feat no one had accomplished until now.

He could picture the headline clearly: "Man Tamer of Manhattan Purrs Like Kitten" for this reporter. Okay, he'd come up with something a little more catchy before he submitted his article to the editor, but time was on his side.

It had taken a busload of flowers and much sweet talking, something he wasn't particularly comfortable doing. Derek preferred the direct approach for women and assignments, but he wanted this interview bad, so he tried the subtle path.

In the end, it had worked—on Amanda Dillon's assistant.

He picked up the photo of the blond performer and studied the image. She didn't look much like a "Man Tamer" or hater for that matter, although rumors told otherwise. Her blue eyes seemed a bit too reserved, evasive even. Her erect posture belied the softness he sensed in her face. She was a puzzle he looked forward to solving before he exposed her to the world.

After all, that was his job.

Derek recalled the warnings he'd gotten from peers when he'd asked for the assignment. A few of his colleagues told how they'd managed to get close enough to ask the "ice queen" out to dinner. All had been coldly rebuffed.

Apparently, she preferred her own company to that of others, taking long walks in Central Park, visiting the Met whenever a new exhibit opened, and lunching at her favorite restaurant, Le Bernardin on 51st.

She didn't give interviews. She didn't date and from what he could gather, with the exception of Wendy Cole, the woman had no friends. If there were secret lovers in her life, the men remained tight-lipped. He arched a brow.

Maybe she didn't like men.

Derek frowned. His gaze stroked over her full breasts and slightly rounded hips, taking in their feminine curve with rapt attention. His nostrils flared as his cock stirred behind the zipper of his trousers. That would be a pity, especially now that he looked forward to being the one to do the taming.

Perhaps all that kept her from saying yes was the right approach.

Derek sat back in his leather chair, his fingers steepled beneath his chin. How could he approach this woman without giving her reason to be defensive? He rocked back and forth, resting his calfskin-clad feet on the edge of his maple desk. His mind wandered in a thousand different directions as he picked and discarded idea after idea.

Damn, there had to be a way into her inner sanctum. One no one else had bothered to explore. He sat up, popping the video he'd purchased from one of the show's participants into a nearby VCR. Still embarrassed by his onstage antics, the man had only been too eager to help him.

Derek watched the tape with a reporter's eyes, looking for any sign of weakness or unexplored opening. He focused on Amanda's smooth and fluid movements, watching how she used a coin on a chain to place the men on stage in a trance. The coin twirled back and forth, flashing in the stage lights, guided by her long slender fingers.

Derek shifted as he imagined those same fingers skimming over his chest and wrapping around his thick cock. He groaned, pulling at the fabric of his trousers to ease his sudden discomfort. Getting into her inner sanctum began to take on a whole new meaning for him. He expelled a heavy breath. Perhaps he had a bit more than just a professional interest in Ms. Amanda Dillon, but he'd keep it in check.

He always did. The women Derek dated knew the rules. He didn't lie to them, because he didn't have to.

On the video, the men's gazes dimmed, glazing over, while their lids dropped closed. Amanda's hypnotic voice spilled out, calm and soothing, weaving them deeper and deeper under her spell. Derek blinked, as he realized he'd almost gone under with them.

Damn, she was good . . . for a fraud.

In an instant, Derek knew what he would do. A smile creased his face and he clasped his hands together, rubbing them in anticipation. The way was clear. Time to meet Ms. Amanda Dillon on her home turf. He smiled as his eyes frisked over her body, looking forward to the day when his hands could do the same.

TWO

Amanda stood off to the side of the stage, house lights turned up so she could see the audience. As always, women made up 90 percent of the crowd.

The first thirty minutes of the show concentrated on mesmerism tricks. She told people about their past, predicted their future, all while holding them captivated, and more than a little curious about how she'd done it.

The audience gladly participated, but Amanda knew what they really wanted. Each night the crowd grew more restless in anticipation of her hypnosis segment. Her act had turned into a monster and she saw no way to kill it, not even with angry villagers and torches.

Her gaze scanned the group. In her mind, she'd already singled out four of the men she'd pick for tonight's performance. They easily stood out among the rest, their arrogant demeanor screaming for attention. Amanda smiled. She'd give them all the attention they could handle and then some.

She skimmed the group, searching for her fifth victim—eh—participant. Her eyes locked on to a man dressed in black trousers and a crisp white shirt. He sat quietly, observing her intently with his silvery-gray gaze. His black jacket hung casually over a crossed leg.

Amanda's heart thumped and skidded to a halt, taking her breath with it. The man was gorgeous, but not in the normal Neanderthal kind of way. His build was trim, but firm. With the body of a triathlete, he sat loose limbed, his gaze locked to hers, yet completely aware of his surroundings. Almost as if he could leap into action at a moment's notice.

Geez girl, he's not a superhero. That thought did little to lesson his impact.

His dark sable hair held glints of salt, even though his aquiline features told her he wasn't much older than thirty-five. But it was his eyes that held Amanda. Like piercing storm clouds, they flashed, giving her a glimpse of the man beneath.

And oh, what a man.

Her heart stammered, and then raced as she took a deep shuddering breath. Heat flooded her face, trailing down her body, licking at her nipples, before settling in her groin. It had been . . . had been . . . well forever, since she'd experienced this kind of reaction to a man.

Excitement and fear battled inside Amanda as she forced herself to look away. *You're a professional, remember?*

Amanda grinned. For purely selfish reasons, she'd just found her fifth participant. She moistened her suddenly dry mouth and made her way back to center stage where a bottle of water awaited her. She loosened the cap and took a drink before placing the bottle on the hardwood floor.

"Ladies and gentlemen, if I could have your attention, please." She spoke into her cordless headpiece mike that could be flicked on and off by a control button at her waist.

The crowd hushed as tension filled the room. Amanda smiled.

"I've chosen tonight's participants. Notice I didn't say willing," she added and the crowd exploded with laughter.

"When I point to you, please quickly come forward to the stage."

Amanda made a big show of pointing to each man. One particular he-man type shook his head in denial. "Oh come on, tiger, I won't hurt you," she purred.

Ego warred with good sense. Lucky for Amanda the former won out. It always did, she thought wryly. She saved the best for last as the spotlight spun around the room waiting for her to make her final choice. It wasn't difficult. She'd known all along whom she wanted onstage next to her.

Amanda pointed, singling out the man with the silvery-gray gaze. She crooked her finger and beckoned him to come to her. His lips quirked and he arched a brow in challenge. For a second she thought he'd refuse, but then just as quickly he smiled and stood, making his way forward.

Amanda released a breath she hadn't known she'd been holding. She actually felt relief. Why it mattered so much that this man participate, she didn't know. But it did. It was as if his presence brought her back to life, reminding her why she'd become a performer in the first place. Exhilaration flooded her, filling the empty well where her creativity had been housed.

She returned his smile as he stepped onto the stage, rearranging the men until her last pick stood next to her.

Big mistake.

Heat rolled from his body in waves, pounding her with unexpected warmth, while his woodsy masculine scent teased her senses. Amanda could feel his hot gaze sliding over her face and down her length, pausing at her aching breasts before moving lower.

All the attention made her wet and needy. She fought the urge to cross her arms over her chest.

If he kept this up, she wouldn't be able to concentrate on anything other than her body's reaction to his nearness. Moving him had definitely been a mistake. The man shifted, drawing himself a few inches closer to her. Amanda's body tingled in feminine awareness, before sounding tornado-like warnings.

Too late.

With trembling fingers, Amanda reached into her pocket and pulled out her coin on a chain. One of many devices she used to place people under hypnosis, this item seemed to work best during a performance. She glanced at each man's face to assure she had his undivided attention.

The gray-eyed man's gaze smoldered in undisguised appreciation. How could she make it through the show if he continued to look at her that way?

Forcing herself to focus, Amanda raised her trembling hand in the air and let the coin slip down until it could spin in the spotlight. "Gentlemen, I want you to listen to my voice, while you look at the coin. Watch how the light reflects off the surface like sunshine on a lake."

Amanda flicked her wrist, causing the coin to spin back and forth. "Soon you'll find yourselves unable to look away and that's okay. You're safe in the light. Nothing can harm you."

She glanced at the men, checking their responsiveness. Many control freaks were somnambulists. These types of people were so highly suggestible that they'd do almost anything she asked. The key was discovering the line in the sand they would not cross.

Amanda continued. "Your eyes may start to water or you may find yourself feeling the urge to swallow. These things are natural. Just allow them to happen."

Unconsciously her gaze sought the man beside her. His concentration appeared locked on the coin as he shifted his weight. She allowed herself to take a moment to look at him. He really did have beautiful eyes, framed with decadently long lashes. It would take Amanda a bottle of mascara to create the same effect. Up close, his face seemed a deeper tan, as if he'd spent days lounging on a beach somewhere.

Amanda pictured him in a small pair of trunks, his lean

muscular form spread out on a blanket across white powdered sand. On the other hand, perhaps he sunbathed nude. The thought caused her to blink and gently squeeze her legs together to stave off the ache. The subtle movement only made things worse.

She followed the fascinating crinkles around his silvery gray eyes, which told her he laughed a lot, to the sensuous swipe of his mouth. Amanda forced back a groan as she imagined exactly how deadly those lips could be to her senses if she allowed him access to her body.

Amanda tore her gaze away from the man. Several of the other men stood, eyes drooping, their breathing slow, steady and deep. She continued her induction. "Your eyelids are getting heavy. It's getting harder and harder to keep them open. When you're ready, and only when you're ready, allow them to close."

The docile tones she used loosened the last of their resistance. Within a couple of minutes all the men had their eyes closed. The muscles in their faces relaxed as the last of the tension left their bodies.

Normally at this point she'd ask the men to do something highly embarrassing to prove they were under trance, but for some reason Amanda couldn't bring herself to make the man standing next to her quack like a duck.

She bit back a curse. She'd never allowed anyone to get under her skin the way this man had. Someone backstage coughed, snapping her out of her reflection. The audience remained quiet, waiting for her next move.

Amanda signaled to a stagehand, who brought five chairs up on stage. She turned to the men before her. "I want you all to open your eyes and walk carefully to the chairs and take a seat."

Simultaneously, the men opened their eyes and strode over to the waiting chairs. Amanda waited until the last one sat then turned to the audience. She still couldn't believe she was about to do this. She'd never changed her show for anyone before. Heck, Amanda had never even considered it.

"Ladies and gentlemen, I'm going to do something a little different tonight. Instead of having these fine gentlemen woo me at the same time, I've decided to bring them up individually."

A couple of anticipatory gasps rang out from the audience followed by encouraging applause.

Derek was damn glad he'd placed a pebble in his shoe before coming up on stage. His toe would probably hurt for a week, but the pain was a small price to pay to keep from falling under hypnosis while Amanda spoke. Up close, she was even more striking than the photograph. Derek battled with his natural urges while standing next her.

The stage lights highlighted her velvety golden hair and soft features, which shone through despite the stage makeup. Bright blue eyes with a luscious red mouth that pouted even when she didn't try to. Amanda looked almost fragile beneath the glaring spotlight and much younger than he'd initially anticipated.

Her body was curved like a woman should be. Her breasts were full and achingly touchable. At one point, Derek shoved his hands into his pockets to keep from reaching out.

Amanda's hips flared and rounded while her generous bottom beckoned to be touched, caressed—stroked. It would be a miracle if he managed to keep his cock in his pants long enough to strip her of her secrets and write this story.

She'd just varied her performance. Derek didn't know why she had changed tack, but it immediately made him wary. He was prepared for the performance he'd viewed on the video, but Amanda spoke to the audience about one-on-one.

Personally, he was more than ready to do one-on-one with Ms. Amanda Dillon, although he'd prefer that act to be private. Professionally, Derek wasn't at all sure he was ready to cross swords with her. What if she discovered his deception? She was a trained hypnotist who should be able to recognize a trance state, or lack thereof, at fifty paces.

Unless the entire act was a fraud like he initially suspected. The thought of a nice, hot, juicy scandal fired his blood, almost as much as the woman standing before him.

Covertly, Derek glanced at the men beside him. There was no mistaking the glazed look in their eyes. The men were under hypnosis. If they were faking it, he'd eat his Italian loafers.

Perhaps she wasn't a fraud after all.

Amanda chose that moment to summon him over to her side. Derek's heart rate shot to the stratosphere. He'd practiced gazing without really seeing in the mirror. In theory, he'd done well, but this wasn't theory any longer.

Amanda asked the man in the black slacks to come to her. He stood in a smooth motion and all but glided across the stage. Amazing for a man who was at least six feet tall. His fluid muscles bunched and stretched like a great wolf striding toward her. For a heartbeat, Amanda felt the overwhelming urge to run. It wasn't as if he was going to pounce on her onstage.

The thought sent a ripple of awareness racing through her. Once again she considered how long it had been since she'd felt anything other than annoyance for a member of the opposite sex. Amanda couldn't recall. This meant one thing. It had been too long.

The man stopped in front of her, his gray gaze unfocused. He looked relaxed, but something about his appearance disturbed her. She looked again. His chest rose and fell in steady, deep rhythms. Amanda ignored the niggle of unease at the back of her mind. He was under like the others, maybe just not as deep.

For some reason the realization brought a mixture of joy

and sadness to Amanda. Part of her wished he wasn't under trance. She shook her head to clear it and continued, knowing his being hypnotized was for the best. The truth was Amanda didn't think she could handle the focus of that gray gaze directly. It was too powerful. Too sexual. Too male.

"Are you comfortable?" she asked, her voice quivering.

The man nodded slowly.

"Good." Amanda smiled as she focused on his face. *Dang, but he was gorgeous.* "I'm going to ask you to woo me in a moment. I want you to give me everything you've got." She turned and winked at the audience, which brought snickers from the crowd.

"But first I'd like to know your name."

He swayed ever so slightly. Amanda reached out to steady him. Her hand locked onto solid muscle and heated strength. She pulled away as if she'd been burned. Maybe knowing his name wasn't such a good idea. Before she could change her mind, he spoke.

"My name is Derek Armstrong."

The name sounded as strong as he felt. She brushed her fingers along her pants leg and swallowed hard, shoring up her resistance.

"Where do you live, Mr. Armstrong?" Amanda's mouth asked the simple question, but her mind demanded more information. *When's your birthday? Are you married? Would you like to have sex on the stage?*

Her eyes widened as the last thought trampled its way through her mind, along with a cavalcade of others. *You are a professional. Time to start acting like one,* she reminded herself again.

"I live in New York," Derek's voice was as smooth as maple syrup gliding over blueberry pancakes.

Amanda's stomach growled and her nipples tightened. She knew she had to ask him to woo her. It was part of the act, but her common sense told her to back away from the nice wolf before he ate her.

She went on with the show. "Okay, Derek. Woo me."

For a minute, he didn't move. He didn't glance her way. He just stood there, muscles locked, his hands balling up into lightly clenched fists.

Amanda was afraid she'd have to ask again. As soon as the thought flitted through her mind, he moved. Except it wasn't the move she'd been expecting. He slid from in front of her to behind her with such grace that it would've made a ballerina blush.

His hand snaked out around her waist and pulled her close, until her back rested against his wide supportive chest. The curve of her bottom greeted his thighs. She could feel the ridge of his erection pressing against her lower back. The move sent gooseflesh rising over Amanda's arms.

"He's smooth," she said in a shaky voice to the audience.

His mouth pressed sensually against her ear while his breath disturbed her neatly coifed hair. "I want to take you—for long walks in the park. Lunches at Le Bernardin and shopping at Tiffany's."

How did he know she liked to have lunch at Le Bernardin? She opened her mouth to ask. His lips skimmed her ear, erasing the question from her mind. Amanda shuddered and her nipples pebbled, raking across the lace of her bra with every inhalation.

What had he whispered? Oh, yeah, Tiffany's.

"He has good taste, folks. We're talking exquisite jewelry here." Amanda giggled nervously, wondering how much more she could take before she begged him to sleep with her. She flicked the mike off so the audience wouldn't hear her pant.

"I want to see your laughter first thing in the morning and your beautiful face glowing with passion as I make you come last thing at night." His fingers splayed across her stomach possessively, pulling her in a notch tighter.

The crowd gasped.

Amanda didn't care.

Heat radiated from his touch, sending warmth searing through her body, lighting up her nerve endings like a roman candle on the Fourth of July.

Amanda couldn't move, couldn't breathe. Refused to think. She should push him away. He'd taken over the show, her senses, with a few well-placed lines, and she'd willingly allowed him to do so.

The only problem was the audience couldn't hear his hypnotic voice. So the performance was just for her. Jealousy wrapped comfortably around possessiveness swirled inside her. Suddenly Amanda didn't want to share, so she did the only thing she could think of, the only thing that would stave off the panic threatening to capsize her. Amanda flicked on her microphone and summoned the other men from their chairs, asking them to woo her too.

The men began the same routine. Some sang while others recited poetry; all the while Derek refused to release his hold. Amanda fought to concentrate. The audience let out catcalls and loud applause, letting her know exactly how much they were enjoying the *show*.

But this wasn't a show to Amanda.

Derek continued whispering exactly what he'd like to do to her in her ear. She'd never been given a tongue bath before but it sounded intriguing coming from his lips. With each new suggestion, Amanda's breath hitched. The man must have memorized the Kama Sutra. His words alone were about to cause her to have an orgasm.

She needed to distance herself. Amanda tried to step away. Derek's grip tightened again. She covered the microphone with her hand, forgetting all about the button at her waist.

"You have to let me go or we'll both embarrass ourselves."

He paused, as a flicker of understanding crossed his face, before fading. "I was only wooing you."

Amanda closed her eyes. In the flourish of passionate

words, she'd forgotten she had commanded him to woo her. Of course, he was in trance like the rest of the men. That fact had slipped her mind, until now.

Heat flooded her face. *What had she been thinking?* Carnal images of twining bodies flashed in her mind. Okay, she knew what she'd been thinking, but that didn't excuse her behavior.

She twisted until she could see Derek's gray eyes. Hunger the likes of which she'd never experienced gnawed at her. For one second, her gaze locked to his lips, fanning the flames of her need to brush fire. Amanda blinked as the panic she'd been holding back struck. She shoved against his grip. This time Derek released. And there was no doubt that if he had not released her, she wouldn't have escaped.

She faced him, her hand still on her mike. "You may stop wooing me now."

His nostrils flared, but his expression remained unreadable. If he weren't under trance, Amanda would have sworn her request had angered him. She glanced down at the front of his trousers. A ridge of hard flesh pressed against the fabric, giving her a clear view of his impressive erection.

She licked her lips and stepped away. Her gaze darted nervously to the audience and back to his trousers. "You may take a seat, Derek," she instructed, her voice sounding breathless.

His lips curved into a wicked grin. "As you wish."

Derek almost growled as he strode back to the seat at the edge of the stage. The other participants continued their outlandish idea of winning Amanda over. Didn't they see she wasn't responding to their attempts? He sat, which wasn't easy in his current condition.

He'd made a mistake grabbing and holding Amanda. Her fresh scent and warm body threw his hormones into overdrive. Derek felt like a teenager around her, unable to keep his hands to himself. He wanted to lay bare what he had managed to detect. Her soft curves now branded him, burned into his flesh from the too-close contact.

Amanda's lips all but begged to be kissed. If they hadn't been on stage, he would have indulged them. Damn, what was the matter with him? Women were plentiful in his life. He didn't need one more. Of course, his shaft wasn't convinced. He sat on the chair, attempting to cool the blood raging through his body.

He couldn't afford to cross the line into the field of emotion. He tensed as he realized how close he'd come to doing just that. Many washed-up careers lay there. Derek vowed his wouldn't be next.

Amanda Dillon was a story. A very sexy, desirable, and intriguing story, but a story nonetheless. He'd do well to remember that fact.

The show drew to a close and Amanda once again stood before the men on stage. She gazed at their faces, judging their level of trance, and then began her countdown to bring them out of hypnosis.

One by one, the men awoke. They glanced around the stage, blinking, taking in their surroundings. Amanda watched closely, her gaze fixating on Derek as a bit of regret stung her. Did she regret placing him under hypnosis or was it because once he awoke he'd no longer be enamored with her?

Amanda wasn't sure. All the men on stage stretched and yawned. All but Derek. She frowned, signaling for the stagehand to retrieve the video copies for the participants while she stepped forward to check on Derek. His breathing was even, yet his eyes remained closed.

She clicked off her mike. "Derek, I want you to awaken." No response.

Amanda glanced around at the audience, who came to their feet in a standing ovation. Her eyes widened as panic began to set in. *Why wasn't he awake?* Her gaze scanned the perimeter of the stage. She caught Wendy's attention. Her assistant stepped onto the stage nonchalantly.

"He won't wake up," Amanda stated calmly, as fear worked its way up her spine.

Wendy's eyes practically bugged out of her skull. "What do you want me to do?" She slid a glance to Derek, her expression perplexed.

"I'm not asking you to carry him off stage. All you have to do is smile, wave, and then take him to my dressing room. I'll finish waking him there."

"What if you can't?"

Amanda felt the color drain from her face. "What do you mean, what if I can't?"

"I just wondered what we'd do with him if you can't wake him up."

"We won't have to worry about it," Amanda said, her voice firm, despite her trembling hands.

Wendy nodded, grasping Derek by an arm. She smiled and waved at the audience on cue. "Come on, handsome, I'll take care of you."

Something suspiciously like jealousy hit Amanda in the stomach, her insides knotting at her assistant's overly familiar tone.

Wendy walked a few feet from Amanda, and then turned. "Has this ever happened to you before?"

"Never." Amanda frowned.

Wendy glanced at Derek, and then back at Amanda. "Well, if you're going to have someone following you around and wooing you for a while, it doesn't hurt that he looks like a movie star."

Amanda's gaze flicked to Derek's handsome face, her body responding instantly with a slow, steady ache. Returning her attention to Wendy, her eyes narrowed. "It doesn't help either."

Three

Derek allowed Wendy to lead him backstage. He wobbled occasionally for effect, although it wasn't difficult with the pebble stabbing him in the foot. His plan was going better than he'd anticipated. Wendy walked him to a door marked with Amanda's name. She opened the door and pushed him inside. The flowers he'd sent Amanda filled the room. He smiled to himself, pleased that she'd kept them.

"Please have a seat."

"Where is my love, Amanda?" he asked, fighting to keep a straight face.

Wendy's hazel eyes bulged with what looked like panic, before narrowing in suspicion. "You seem familiar. Do I know you?"

"I don't think so," he said, dropping his gaze to his hands. Had she recognized his voice? He'd spoken to this woman on multiple occasions. Surely, she'd say if she did. The moment stretched on, grating his nerves.

"Hmm, I guess you're right. Oh well, Amanda will be here any second. You can sit on the couch and wait for her." She patted his arm and spoke slowly as if he couldn't understand English.

Derek nodded and sat on the tiny blue couch that had

seen better days. Wendy assessed him for several minutes, and then turned away, a smile curling her lips.

The second Amanda's assistant turned her back Derek scanned the room. All the items in Amanda's dressing room appeared worn. Odd, considering her act raked in the money. What was she doing with the cash? He made a mental note to find out.

For now, he needed to get back into character and play his part. He leaned back, his large frame taking up over half the navy couch. He gazed, unfocused, at a point on the wall. Several minutes later the door burst open and Amanda Dillon entered the room. He responded to the crash, but just barely.

"I thought I told you to get rid of these flowers," she snapped at Wendy.

Derek flinched.

"Right away, boss." Wendy saluted and clicked her heels together.

Amanda closed her eyes for a second. "I'm sorry, Wendy. I didn't mean to bark at you. I'm just freaking out."

"I know." She smiled and squeezed Amanda's shoulder in silent support.

Amanda touched her hand briefly, then rushed forward and dropped to her knees in front of him. Her fingertips brushed Derek's legs before settling on the couch beside him. The sight had the muscles in his thighs tensing. It didn't take much imagination on Derek's part to realize what else this position would be good for. He bit the inside of his mouth to keep from groaning aloud.

She pressed forward, parting his legs to accommodate her body. Derek started reciting the states and capitals in his mind, before picturing his grandmother in her underdrawers. He inwardly cringed at the latter, but he was desperate. Anything to keep his mind off Amanda's head being anywhere near his cock.

"Derek, can you hear me?" she murmured.

He nodded slowly, his gaze turning to her.

"Good." She mirrored his acknowledgment. "I'm going to count to ten, and when I reach the number ten, I want you to wake up feeling refreshed and well rested. Do you understand?"

"Yes." Spontaneously, Derek reached for Amanda's hand and brushed his lips across her knuckles. She quivered.

"What was that for?" she asked, as her mouth dropped open, forming a silent "O."

He smiled, reveling in her reaction to his touch. "I have only just begun to woo you," he warned. "Tell me what you desire when you close your eyes at night—the moment before you drift off to sleep. Is it someone like me, who'd pull you close and tell you everything is going to be all right? Or do you desire unbridled passion, hot and wet, matching the fire I sense inside of you? I can be both." The last words left his mouth like a whispered promise that he intended to keep.

She flushed, awareness flaring in her vibrant blue eyes. Her face went from open to closed as she snatched her hand away. "I'm going to count now. One . . . Two . . . Three . . . Atch-oo. Sorry, allergies." She glanced at the flowers.

Derek inwardly cringed. Just his luck the woman was allergic to flowers. It was his fault she suffered. She began to count again.

Amanda reached the end of her count, with her hand still tingling from where Derek's lips had touched. She expected to see his eyelids flutter and recognition to return, but it didn't happen.

He looked no different from when they'd started. His breathing remained steady, his gaze unchanged. The only discernible difference she could note was the slash of color in his cheeks.

What am I going to do now?

Her heart raced painfully in her chest. She couldn't send

him home in this condition. There had to be a way of waking him. Her mind scattered as she considered all her options. The same answer came back repeatedly.

She was responsible for him until she could wake him. Amanda needed to take him home with her so she could consult her hypnotherapy journals, making sure she hadn't missed anything. The thought of having this man in her home both frightened and thrilled her.

She turned to Wendy, unable to close her expression before her assistant noticed. "I'm going to take Derek home with me so that I can continue to work on him."

Her assistant's brow shot to her hairline. "Continue to work on him, eh?"

Amanda ignored her remark. "I'm sure this is simply a temporary setback. Everything will be fine."

"Who are you trying to convince? Me or yourself?"

"Wendy, we'll have that discussion later. Right now I need you to help me get Derek back to my apartment."

Wendy released a heavy breath, blowing her bangs up at the same time. "Well, I suppose it could be worse."

Amanda snorted. "You're kidding, right? How so?"

"He could be a troll, instead of drop-dead gorgeous."

"At the moment, I don't think his appearance ranks as the most important thing here, do you?"

"I guess not," she said begrudgingly. "But look at him, his appearance certainly doesn't hurt."

"No, it does—" Amanda spoke before she realized what she was about to agree with. She clamped her mouth shut.

Oblivious, Wendy continued. "He's not just a side of beef. He's like the whole cow. Fine. Fine. Fine."

"Enough! I don't want to talk about it anymore. You know, he *can* hear you. The man's not deaf." Amanda scowled.

They both glanced at Derek, who sat unblinking on the couch.

"Yeah, I know he can hear me, but he won't remember

anything once you wake him up. Pity, really." An evil grin crossed her friend's face.

"No! Whatever it is, the answer is no."

A smile tugged at Wendy's mouth as she eyed her boss.

"Don't say a single word. Not one. I mean it," Amanda warned.

Wendy smirked. "I wouldn't dream of it, boss. Besides, it would be way too easy." She laughed, grasping her flat belly.

"Laugh now. We'll see what happens the next time you come to me wanting a raise."

Wendy wiped the tears from her eyes. "I can't help it. The whole thing is funny."

Amanda's lips twitched.

"It holds such delicious possibilities," she added, winking at Derek.

"Are you implying that I would take advantage of Mr. Armstrong's condition?"

"Nope, of course not. I'm implying I would if I were you."

An hour later, Amanda opened the door to her apartment and flipped on the lights. For some reason she was nervous. Her gaze darted around the room to make sure she hadn't left anything lying about.

White covers draped her couch and two chairs. Photography books were scattered across her coffee table. Her kitchen nook remained tidy, because she never bothered to cook, what with the city being filled with so many good restaurants.

She stepped aside and asked Derek to enter. He did—with a big smile on his face.

"So this is your home," he stated more than asked. "It's nice. It smells like you."

Amanda frowned and took a whiff. At least it didn't

stink. She shut the door behind him and locked it, before turning to face him. She needed to go through her journals, but first she needed a shower to clear her head.

"You'll be sleeping in here if I can't get you out of this trance. I know it's not much. They claim it's a second bedroom, but my bet is on a closet. There's a tiny guest bathroom there."

He laughed, his gray eyes twinkling. "I'm sure it will be fine, but where will you sleep?"

She licked her suddenly dry lips before answering. "My bedroom is through there." She pointed to a door off to the left of the room. "If you need anything just call."

"I wouldn't want to disturb you."

"It's not a problem. You won't be disturbing me. I'll be researching the best way to help you. Besides, I don't sleep very well anyhow."

He tilted his head, his expression curious.

"Nope." She shrugged. "I consider myself a functioning insomniac." Amanda laughed.

"You're not the only one. I tend to get up in the middle of the night and work."

"I suppose we can keep each other company then."

He grinned. "I'd like that."

Derek settled into the little room Amanda used as a guest bedroom. She'd been right when she pegged it for a closet. He hoped like hell that the space didn't make him claustrophobic before he got what he needed for the article.

Dotted like tiny bushes across a vast landscape, pictures covered the light green walls. Some were of Amanda as a child, smiling, two front teeth missing, her pigtails daring to be yanked. A few had her dressed like a sorcerer, including the hat and wand. She looked happy.

A tinge of guilt thumped across Derek's chest. He pushed it aside.

The photos continued through the years. Amanda graduating from high school and going on to college. Shortly thereafter the tone of the pictures changed, grew dark, shadowed. Smiles became less and less frequent.

One of the pictures showed Amanda next to a man that he assumed was her father. The man's head dipped indulgently to the girl, but never lost the sadness lurking in his eyes.

Derek frowned. He knew the names of Amanda's parents, but not much more. Her father passed away eight years ago, not long after the photo had been taken. Since they didn't invest in her show, he'd ignored them, dismissing them as unimportant with regard to his story angle.

Now he wasn't so sure.

He rubbed his chin. The sound of his nails scraping over newly formed stubble filled the silence. His lips quirked. Maybe Amanda would allow him to use her razor. He shook his head in amusement as he pictured her expression when he asked.

As he suspected, there was more to Amanda Dillon than met the eye.

The sound of a shower running in the distance caused Derek to turn. An image of Amanda's stark-ass naked body standing under the spray scored his senses like long fingernails scraping down his bare back. Would she stand facing the water or have her back turned so the droplets curved around her lush bottom?

Both images had Derek's cock leaping to attention. He ran his fingers through his hair, while he worked on tempering his thoughts. With her in the shower, he had the perfect opportunity to make a call. He reached into his jacket pocket and pulled out his cell phone.

Several seconds later, his editor Dave Mason answered the phone.

"Where in the hell are you? I've been trying to reach you all evening."

Derek glanced over his shoulder. Amanda's door remained

closed with the shower still running. "I'm in Amanda Dillon's home."

"You're what?"

"I'm in Amanda Dillon's home. It's a long story. I'll explain later. Do me a favor, Dave. Check out Amanda's parents."

"It's not my job to do your research for you," he grumbled.

"Just do it. Oh, and get ready to save the cover page for me." Derek pressed the off button and shoved the phone back into his jacket.

He stepped into the living room and decided to explore. Amanda didn't have much in the way of furnishings. A couch, a chair, a tiny table and chairs that made up the dining portion of the room, and a spotless kitchenette. Derek's lips tilted. She wasn't much of a domestic goddess.

Four plants sat on her tiny windowsill. They looked to be herbs of some kind. He rounded the coffee table, glancing at her choice of reading material, noting the book on photography. So maybe they had something in common after all—other than lust.

He walked to a small built-in bookcase. The shelves were lined with psychology books, along with hypnotherapy and mesmerism items. Crystals hung from chains and small candleholders housed tea lights. Everything here had a purpose. Nothing but the photos on the wall in the other room seemed personal. Almost as if she didn't want to be reminded of the past.

Derek frowned. The door creaked open behind him and Amanda stood there in a pair of faded denims and a red T-shirt. Her feet were bare, revealing her brightly painted toes, and her hair was wrapped in a fluffy pink towel. Her gaze locked on him. She tensed for a moment then smiled.

"Can I get you a cup of tea?" she asked, heading for the small kitchen before he could reply. "I always have one after a show. It settles my nerves."

"Please."

Her faint soapy fresh smell filled the room, followed by a richer floral scent. She must have applied lotion. Derek imagined the glide of her hands slathering the rich cream over miles of silky white skin. He swallowed hard, before moving to the window. This was turning into his toughest assignment yet.

Amanda approached a few minutes later carrying a teapot on a tray. She placed the tray onto the coffee table and beckoned him to sit. Derek did so reluctantly. His fingers itched to remove the towel. He wanted to run his hands through her thick blond hair to see if it was as soft as it appeared.

Everything about Amanda screamed sex, even though he knew that wasn't the look she was going for. He bit back a smile. She handed him a cup of tea before reaching for her own and then tucking her feet beneath her on the couch.

Her blue gaze pierced him, daring him to reveal his secrets. He couldn't and wouldn't, but it was tempting. Like this intriguing woman. Damn. Could she get any more kissable? Derek didn't think so. She took a sip of tea. Her tongue darted out to catch a wayward drop. He tensed, envious of the stray droplet.

"We better get started." She rose, retrieving her hypnosis journals from the shelves.

For the next three days, Amanda tried everything in the book to "wake" him up: soft inductions, hard inductions, short scripts, long scripts. He actually felt sorry for her.

"I don't know why it's not working." She scratched the side of her head, frustration sneaking into her voice as she sat back. She grabbed her cup of tea, the one she had every night, and took a sip.

"Do you have any idea how beautiful you are?" he asked, surprising even himself.

She blinked, then colored.

"I'm sure you hear it all the time, but it's true." He

leaned forward. "You leave me breathless." He spoke the words effortlessly, feeling their meaning for the first time.

Looking increasingly uncomfortable, Amanda set the cup down. "It's late. I'd better fix us something to eat. You're probably hungry and I know I am." Her gaze strayed back to him.

Derek allowed her to escape. She obviously needed to distance herself. Over the past few days, they'd grown more aware of each other and their increasing attraction. It was palpable and pulsed in the air like an electric current whenever their eyes met.

A heartbeat later, Derek rose and followed her into the kitchen. They'd been ordering takeout in the evenings, so his surprise at her culinary offer must have shown on his face, because she commented.

"I know the kitchen doesn't look used and it isn't often, but I can cook."

He grinned, purposely crowding her with his body to see the flare of awareness spark in her eyes. "I never said you couldn't."

She pulled fresh vegetables from the small refrigerator and then grabbed a cutting board. She lined the vegetables up before slipping a paring knife from its holder. Amanda began to chop with efficiency. Derek used her distraction to move behind her. He leaned into her hair and inhaled.

It was like smelling the first spring rain in the New England countryside. Fresh and crisp, lightly sweet with hints of sunshine.

"Ow!"

His head shot up at her cry and he glanced over her shoulder. Amanda held her bleeding finger with her other hand.

"Are you all right?" He moved to her side and glanced around the kitchen for a rag to stop the bleeding. There was none. His gaze strayed to the fancy linen napkins they were going to use for dinner.

"I'm sorry," he murmured a second before whipping one of the napkins out from under the plates. Dishes skidded across the counter.

"Hey!" Her brow furrowed. "Stop and watch."

Derek froze in mid-motion, his heart skittering in his chest. His gaze went from her face, which was the picture of concentration, to her bleeding finger.

Amanda's breathing deepened and she closed her eyes. Within a minute, the blood flow slowed. She opened her eyes and continued breathing deep. Moments later it had stopped.

"H-How did you do that?" Genuine awe filled Derek's voice.

"Self-hypnosis." Amanda smiled.

"That's all."

She shrugged. "What can I say? I'm good at my day job."

The understatement of the century, from what Derek could see. The words leaving her mouth were followed quickly by a frown as her gaze met his.

Derek forced himself not to react to her, even though he knew what she was thinking. Amanda had forgotten why he was there. A slip of the knife brought it all back. She was beginning to doubt her abilities.

Part of him longed to correct her. Pull her into his arms and kiss the frown from her face. The reporter inside denied him the pleasure on both fronts.

"Where are your Band-Aids?" he asked, forcing his mind away from his conscience.

She nodded toward her bedroom. "They're in the bath-room medicine cabinet."

He turned and strode to her bedroom. Derek pushed the door open and stopped in surprise. He'd expected her room to be frilly, girly, perhaps soft and feminine.

Instead, it was made up of hard masculine lines with its mahogany bed frame and hunter green walls. A matching mahogany dresser sat across from the bed. A few more pho-tos dotted its top, along with the coin she used to hypnotize the group each night.

He ran his hand over the crisp white linens covering the bed. They were soft as silk beneath his touch. He imagined Amanda lying in the center of the bed. Her blond hair tossed wildly over the pillow. Her naked body covered only by a thin sheet. Derek licked his lips, pulling his hand away from the bed.

Focus, man.

He continued into the bathroom and found the Band-Aids in the medicine cabinet like she'd said. He grabbed a couple before tucking the box back into the cabinet. Lotions and perfumes lined a thin glass shelf, along with a hairbrush and comb. These were the only feminine touches in an other-wise starkly black-and-white bathroom.

She simply wasn't fitting in the easy box he'd con-structed. Derek returned to the kitchen and bandaged her finger. She washed the knife, checking to ensure the vegeta-bles hadn't been splattered with blood before continuing with her task.

"You don't have to stand here and watch me," she said, impatience and something else he couldn't quite identify filling her voice.

He propped a shoulder against a cabinet, crossing his arms over his chest. "I don't mind. I like watching you." Shockingly, it was the truth. He couldn't seem to keep his eyes off her, and barely managed not to touch.

Amanda's breath hitched, but she didn't look at him, so she missed the smile curving Derek's lips.

She finished chopping the veggies and then turned to him. "If you're going to stand there like a lump then I'm going to put you to work."

He straightened.

"Dig into the freezer and see if you can find the steaks.

They'll have to be defrosted, but it shouldn't hurt the flavor too much."

Derek did as he was told. The whole scene seemed so *domestic*. Comfortable even. He'd never really done the domestic thing with a woman. He tended to be more at ease with bed sport. As long as emotions stayed out of the equation, he was good. But with Amanda it was different. Easier.

It surprised him how much he enjoyed helping her with dinner. They worked in the small kitchen like a finely oiled machine, moving fluidly around each other to reach for various items. Derek made sure to brush against her a couple of times, just so he could hear her breath catch.

Forty-five minutes later dinner was done. He helped Amanda set the table and then opened a bottle of wine he'd spotted in one of the cabinets earlier.

Her gaze strayed to the bottle. "Derek, I really don't think—"

"It'll compliment the dinner, Amanda. Just have a seat and let me take care of you for a while."

She hesitated a moment, then sat. Derek grabbed a candle from the bookshelf and slid it onto the center of the table. He found two crystal wineglasses and brought them along with the bottle over to the table. He poured the wine while Amanda watched.

He handed her a glass, before raising his own. "Here's to a lovely meal and an even lovelier woman."

He lightly tapped her glass then raised the crystal to his lips. She paused, before following suit.

Amanda swallowed a larger swig of wine than she'd intended. Liquid courage was the last thing she needed right now. She found it difficult enough to remember this wasn't a date, and that Derek wasn't here of his own free will. Although he seemed to be doing everything in his power to prove otherwise.

The harsh planes of his face softened in the candlelight, giving him an almost boylike quality. His gray eyes glistened, along with the silver in his hair as he spoke about her coffee table book and his interest in photography with gleeful abandon. His passion was apparent, catching her up and binding her in his fiery orbit. She'd never tire of looking at him.

He truly was a striking man. One that if she were perfectly honest, she found madly attractive. But she couldn't act on that attraction, could she? Amanda took another drink of wine. *Why not?* Her conscience screamed.

Without asking, Derek reached for the bottle of Merlot and refilled her glass. His fingers brushed the back of her knuckles before he returned the bottle to its resting place. Their gazes locked and melded, heating with molten fire and insatiable lust.

Temptation flooded Amanda, drowning her reasons, before washing away the last of her common sense.

Four

Amanda knew she should protest or at least say something as Derek rounded the small table. Her tongue had a mind of its own as it tied her words into knots. Derek's mouth descended gradually, giving her plenty of time to move away. She didn't. She wanted this. Wanted him.

The brush of his firm lips was tender at first, languidly drawing out her reaction before pressing deeper for more. She opened for him like a jack-in-the-box, her tongue springing out to meet his hungrily. The taste of him overwhelmed her, spinning her head faster than the wine ever could.

His drugging kisses were sensual and seasoned. He didn't waste energy or hold back. His lips fed from hers, drinking in her essence, demanding a response. And Amanda did respond. Her fingers sank into his shoulders as she stood on wobbly legs to meet him. Their bodies pressed tightly, scraping and throbbing as they tried to get closer.

Derek's hands grasped her hips and squeezed before sliding around to cup the full globes of her buttocks. Amanda moaned against his mouth as he kneaded and teased. Moisture flooded her panties as his tongue matched his massages. Her head was spinning, as her leg lifted of its own accord and wrapped around his hard thigh.

His erection pulsed and grew behind the zipper of his pants. Like a cat against an unsuspecting leg, Amanda slid her body along his length. It was Derek's turn to groan. He pulled back from the kiss long enough to ravage her ear and neck, nibbling and sucking with just the right pressure.

"I've tried to keep my hands off you, but I can't fight it anymore," he murmured.

Tingles started at the base of Amanda's skull and then shot straight to her toes.

Gasping breaths filled the silence of the room as the remnants of dinner were forgotten. Derek reached around, grasping her thigh a second before lifting Amanda off the ground. Her legs automatically wrapped around his waist as he ground his sex suggestively against hers, before striding toward her bedroom.

They made it as far as the living room wall.

Derek stopped, pressing her against the wall, the weight of his body holding her in place. Muscles bulged in his neck as he leaned back far enough to strip the sweatshirt from her. He groaned. Amanda's breasts came close to spilling out of the lace cups of her bra as she struggled for breath.

He cupped her, threading her nipples between his thumb and forefinger, before taking over with his mouth. The second his lips made contact, Amanda groaned. Her skin was on fire. Like individual notes to a symphony, each caress only added to the pleasure filled discomfort.

"Do you care about your bra?" he asked in a guttural tone.

She shook her head.

Amanda heard material rip a moment before her nipples were released from their bindings, exposed to his heat-seeking mouth and masterful hands. She ground her sex against his, praying for an iota of relief. None came. Her actions only served to ratchet her need a notch higher.

Derek plucked and suckled, devouring her fleshy peaks in complete abandon. Amanda's hands smoothed into his hair, before tightening on the strands so she could pull his head back.

"I-I need more," she growled, unable to recognize her own voice.

His nostrils flared while his gray eyes glistened like liquid mercury. Derek's hands fastened onto the front of her jeans. He deftly unbuttoned the top button before slowly sliding the zipper down, exposing her matching lace panties. He leaned forward and inhaled, closing his eyes in what could have been ecstasy or agony.

"Let's take this in the other room before I take you right here against the wall."

Amanda gulped and nodded, one of the few movements she was currently capable of performing. He scooped her higher onto his hips and walked the short distance into her bedroom.

Derek laid Amanda on the bed gently. His hands slid down the length of her body, brushing over her legs, taking her pants with them. She lay against the white linens clad only in her scrap of underwear. He'd never seen a woman more beautiful or alluring.

He allowed his gaze to take in every curve, every dip. Her nipples puckered, drawing into tiny beads under his perusal. Her skin had tasted like honey against his tongue. He itched to taste her further. The rich smell of sex and arousal hung in the air like an aphrodisiac. He dropped her jeans, before leaning forward to press a kiss upon her abdomen.

She trembled beneath his touch. He glanced at her eyes, which were now shaded by her long lashes. Her rosy lips were parted as she sucked on one finger to try to gain relief. The sight had his cock hardening to the point of pain. He longed to replace her finger with his shaft.

His body shook as he fought for control. Never had he

been so keyed up and anxious to be inside a woman. Something about Amanda Dillon was decidedly different. It wasn't her looks, although they suited him well. It wasn't her fame or reputation. Those attributes were interesting, but not as much as the woman herself.

He growled low in his chest as he reached for her lace panties and tugged them down. His breath caught as he gazed at the bare skin between her legs. For a second he thought he would drool.

"You're killing me here," he murmured to her, while placing a hand over his chest, feigning heart failure.

She laughed.

"I can't wait to taste every last inch of your body and I know exactly where to start."

Amanda's smile faded and she moaned. The finger she'd been nipping trailed from her mouth to her nipple. He tensed, his gaze locking on to her movements. Distracted, Derek fumbled with the belt around his waist.

"Before I lose my head and forget." He reached into his back pocket and pulled out his wallet, extracting a few condoms. From the look she was giving him, he hadn't brought nearly enough.

Amanda made a noise very close to purring. Derek closed his eyes and prayed for strength. "You are a very wicked woman. You know that?"

She smiled. "I've never been called that before. I kind of like it. Maybe it'll replace 'Man Tamer of Manhattan' as my new nickname."

Derek laughed, filing the information away for later use. He slipped his pants down his legs, toeing his shoes and socks off at the same time. "I think it's perfect. Or maybe I'll just call you 'wicked woman.' It can be my private name for you."

He could see the headlines now.

"I can be a *very* wicked woman," she teased.

Hunger filled his body leaving him rapacious. "Show me." He'd worry about the cover story later.

Amanda couldn't believe the daring statements coming out of her mouth. She'd never been a wicked woman in her life, but with Derek, she wanted to be. He brought out the wildness in her. She glanced down at the muscle she'd only felt through clothing until now. He was glorious in his nakedness. Not quite Greek god, but certainly nothing to sneeze at.

Her gaze started at his collarbone, before lingering on his wide expanse of a chest. Hair circled his flat disklike nipples, then didn't reappear until his navel where it squiggled a jagged path down to an impressive erection. Amanda licked her lips. If she were a virgin there would be no way she'd allow that thing anywhere near her, but since she wasn't she intended to feast on every inch of him.

"Keep licking those lips and I'm going to put something there to really wrap your mouth around."

She grinned and arched a brow. "Is that a promise?"

His eyes flashed in warning. "Oh yeah."

"Prove it," she dared.

Derek didn't move where she thought he would. Instead, he dropped to his knees and gently picked up her legs one at a time, dropping them over his shoulders until her knees rested by his ears. He leaned forward and blew air over her bare skin, cooling and heating her at the same time.

Amanda's skin prickled and her breath caught in anticipation. His tongue snaked out of his mouth and he ran it along her hairless seam, pausing at the sensitive bundle of nerves hidden in the folds. Her back arched as he pressed deeper, spearing her, lapping at her hungry flesh.

Blindly she clawed at the covers, anchoring herself in the satiny sheets as he sucked and flicked, continuing to devour her. A steady throb started at her center, building with such intensity that she feared it would wipe away her existence.

Derek tilted her hips then plunged deeper, seeking out her core with his mouth, teeth, and tongue. One last swirl and sanity slipped away. Amanda came on a whimpering cry, while her body stretched taut like a web caught in a breeze.

She couldn't see and the only thing she could hear was the pounding of her heart ricocheting inside her chest. Her breath sawed in and out of her lungs as her body trembled with the last remnants of desire before reaching satiation.

She didn't feel Derek move. One minute her vision returned and she'd seen the ceiling, the next he was staring down at her, a wicked grin covering his face. He wiped her moisture from his chin, then kissed her soundly. Amanda could taste her essence on his tongue, but she didn't care.

Her body was boneless and sinking deeper into the covers as she melted away. The sound of foil ripping reached her ears a second before his shaft pressed into her entrance. The head stretched her, despite the fact she was slick and wet. He slowed, his breath panting in her ear.

"I'm going to try to take my time, but you're so tight and hot and wet that I'm afraid I may not make it."

She grinned then wiggled, causing him to slip another inch inside of her. She gasped as he moved his hips back and forth.

"We've got a long way to go." He winked.

"I'm game if you are." *Who had taken over her mouth and body?*

Derek withdrew, then surged forward, impaling her to the hilt with his impressive length. Amanda cried out as her body stretched to accommodate him. One thrust and he'd put an end to her two years of self-imposed celibacy. Not that she was about to tell Derek that.

When her breathing returned to normal, he started to move. His thrusts were slow at first, lazy motions to reawaken her body. As the tension inside her returned,

Amanda latched onto his shoulders, her fingers skimming over the sinewy muscles in his broad back.

She reached lower, grasping his bottom as he drove into her, rotating his hips for deeper penetration. She matched his rhythm as if they'd been doing this together for a lifetime. Senses rippling, their movements turned fevered, while his kisses turned fierce, delirious.

Amanda clung as the sensations became too much. She sunk her nails into his skin as a cry of release was ripped from her lungs.

Her body milking him ignited primal urges. Derek grunted as his thrusts turned possessive. He wanted this woman. Needed to mean more than a quick fuck to her. He wanted to brand her, mark her somehow, so that there was no mistaking what they'd done. Instead, she'd marked him. Amanda sunk her nails into his flesh like an animal unleashed. He'd have welts if she kept at it, and he'd wear each one proudly.

He bucked under her grip, as the warmth of her body enwrapped him in pulsing contractions. Steel muscles met soft flesh as he fucked her hard. The blood rushed to his ears, creating a dull roar as Derek bellowed out his release, following her into the land of satiation.

Several minutes later, they revived enough to separate. Derek disposed of the condom in the bathroom, and then walked back into the bedroom in time to see Amanda slipping under the covers.

"Would you like some company?" he asked, ready to beg. He'd known it when he walked into the bathroom, but when he returned to see her face it was confirmed. This had been the best sex of his life and he feared it was only the beginning of something better, something deeper that he refused to linger on right now.

Amanda stretched languidly, her blue gaze skimming

over his flesh like a caress. Her pert nipples pressed against the sheets reminding him of his earlier fantasy, except this was better. He responded instinctually. He couldn't do otherwise. His shaft twitched and started to grow, rising again like the Phoenix from ashes.

Amanda's eyes widened as her gaze locked on his sex in what looked to be a cross between fascination and horror. Guilt swept him. He had been more than a little rough on her. He was about to make his excuses and go to the other room when she threw the covers back and beckoned him to join her.

They made love throughout the night, sometimes with their mouths, sometimes with their hands. When the early morning sun peeked into the window, bathing their faces, their bodies were still joined.

Amanda awoke gradually from what felt like a delicious dream. Her body ached in places where she didn't even know she had muscles. She tried to move, but she was pinned in place by something. Her eyes flew open as last night's events erupted in her head. Panic swelled inside her, along with a healthy dose of shame.

She'd taken advantage of a helpless man. *He didn't feel helpless.* "Oh shut up," she mumbled to herself.

"Did you say something?" Derek's voice held a hint of gravel as he kissed her naked shoulder. His arm wrapped around her, squeezing her to his body, as he snuggled deeper.

Tingles of desire swept through Amanda. This wasn't good. And it certainly wasn't sane. "I need to take a shower."

"Care for some company?"

"I, uh, maybe next time," she blurted, then scrambled from his grasp. She had to think. She needed to call Wendy. She'd know what to do.

No!

On second thought, that probably wasn't a good idea. Wendy wouldn't see anything wrong with what happened last night and she'd darn well never let Amanda live it down.

Amanda jumped into the shower after locking the bathroom door. She scrubbed and scrubbed, but couldn't wash away the enjoyment she felt last night while lying in Derek's strong arms. Her body thrummed, sensitive in places it hadn't been for a very long time. Derek had single-handedly given her the best sexual experience of her life.

How was she supposed to top that? And with whom? All good questions she didn't have the answers to.

Under different circumstances, she'd gladly enter into a relationship with this man. He was handsome and charming. He cooked and didn't mind cleaning up. Heck, he was the perfect guy. She frowned, allowing the spray to soak her head.

But given the current situation, she'd be lucky if he didn't have her arrested. Goodness knows she'd probably broken several laws. She wasn't sure which ones, but there had to be several. Amanda groaned.

She needed to get Derek back to his home—back to his life. Four days had passed since the show and nothing had changed. *Except your feelings for the guy.* Amanda cursed. She couldn't have him hanging around her apartment much longer. She was falling for him in a big way.

You already have, her traitorous mind added, stating the obvious.

Maybe he had relatives in the city. If he did, she could take him to their home and it would jog his memory and snap him out of the trance. At least now, she had a sane plan.

Her mind jumped immediately from her new plan to reviewing the events of last night in slow, slow motion.

Amanda's nipples prickled and her breath deepened. She

ran her hand along her arm and over her breasts, before descending between her legs to her slick folds, as she recalled his masterful touch.

She circled her greedy flesh twice feeling it kernel beneath her fingertips. Her body shuddered. It wouldn't take much for her to reach orgasm. Since when had she become a sex fiend?

Since last night, when you slept with Derek Armstrong.

Amanda plucked her swollen nub and then reached for the faucet handle, turning the water to cold. This was insane. She had to be insane. Amanda shivered under the chill until her body cooled off. Too bad the icy spray couldn't reach her heart.

Derek didn't know for sure what Amanda Dillon was doing in the bathroom, but he'd heard muttered curses which gave him a pretty good idea he wasn't going to like it. Damn! What had he done wrong?

He hadn't expected them to make love last night, but they had. He wasn't stupid enough to fool himself into thinking it had been just sex. He'd had sex before—and that wasn't it. He didn't know what to do now. The lines between professional and personal blurred before him.

Derek got out of bed and dressed. He slipped from the bedroom and went into the kitchen. Amanda had enough eggs in her refrigerator to make a couple of omelets. After checking the expiration date on the carton, he found a pan and went to work.

By the time Amanda entered the room, wearing a soft baby blue sweater with deep navy pants, breakfast was served. Her eyes widened in what appeared to be surprise, when she saw the plates. He'd found bread so they had toast and butter to go along with the eggs.

"Have a seat." He pulled the chair out for her.

She sat.

"I thought you might be hungry. I'm famished." He grinned, rounding the table to his chair.

"I made you some tea, but I couldn't recall if you took anything in it."

Amanda opened her mouth as if to say something, but appeared to change her mind. "I drink my tea plain. This"— she gestured to the table—"is lovely. Thank you, Derek. You really didn't need to go to all this trouble."

"It was no trouble. Now, eat up, before the eggs get cold," he urged, raising his cup of tea to his lips.

Amanda took a few bites of the food. Her eyes closed for a second, savoring each bite as she chewed. "Hmm . . ."

Her lovely blue eyes had closed in much the same way when he'd entered her last night. In his mind, Derek could still feel her hot, moist sheath gripping him. Her nails scoring his back and the soft moans she made when she'd climaxed.

"This is delicious." She licked her lips, before smiling at him. "Where did you learn how to cook?"

Her question brought him back to reality. "Thanks. My grandmother taught me everything she knows about cooking."

Her eyes flew open. "Really?" Amanda took another bite, before chasing it with a sip of tea. "Does she live in the area?"

"As a matter of fact, she does."

Amanda smiled. "Wonderful. We'll go there for a visit. Won't that be nice?"

Derek almost choked on his bite of eggs. Going to see his grandmother was a horrible idea. She'd bust his cover the second he walked in her front door.

"Why do you want to visit my grandmother?" he asked, dabbing his mo⸺ ⸺ ⸺ the napkin.

"I thoug⸺ ⸺ ⸺e seeing her would bring back pleasant *memo⸺* ⸺ ⸺

So that was her plan. Amanda thought she'd take him to his grandmother's house and he'd wake up. Trouble was, Derek wasn't ready to "wake up." He was enjoying his time with Amanda too much. He'd play along, because someone under trance wouldn't resist.

"That would be great," he added. Maybe he'd have time to phone Nana Joan beforehand to coach her. Derek snorted silently. Like that was going to happen. She wouldn't lie for him. He'd be lucky if she didn't scold him in front of Amanda for lying.

Amanda grinned. "As soon as we finish here, we'll go."

"Great." He might as well line up in front of the firing squad now.

Amanda dug into her food in earnest, while Derek picked at his, absently moving the eggs around the plate. He'd suddenly lost his appetite.

Five

Derek washed the dishes while Amanda changed her clothes. The phone rang in three quick bursts. The bedroom door remained closed.

"Amanda, phone."

It rang again. He wasn't sure if he should pick it up or not. He wiped his hands on a nearby dish towel and walked the short distance to the cordless.

The phone rang again. Derek looked around for an answering machine, but didn't see one. He glanced over his shoulder one last time at Amanda's door. Still closed, he reached for the phone.

"Hello, Amanda Dillon's residence. May I help you?" Derek asked, his voice raspy.

"Wow! You're still there. I can't believe it," the excited voice on the other end of the line exclaimed.

"What are you doing?"

Derek's head snapped around at the sound of Amanda's chilly voice. "I-I tried to call you, but you didn't answer. The phone was ringing."

Amanda glowered. "Give it to me." She held out her hand.

Derek placed the handset into her palm and then returned to the kitchen to finish the dishes.

Heat rushed to Amanda's face as she placed the receiver to her ear and heard her assistant Wendy talking. She closed her eyes, willing her heart to slow down. She hadn't done anything wrong.

Ha! Nothing wrong! You slept with an audience member—who was still under.

"Hello." She pushed the guilt aside and forced her voice to work.

"Well, well, well . . . what happened last night? Derek sounds a little worse for wear."

Amanda cleared her throat. "It wasn't like that." *Yes, it was.*

"Really? Then tell me what it was like."

She blew out a frustrated breath. Amanda wasn't about to discuss her sex life with Wendy. *Wow, after two years, she actually had a sex life to discuss.* The thought momentarily cheered Amanda up until Wendy asked her next question.

"Did he ever come out of the trance?"

The pit of Amanda's stomach plummeted. She'd taken advantage of a helpless man. She did the only thing she could think of—she fibbed, sort of. "He's a little more coherent." That was an understatement. The man was an animal.

"That's terrific. Are you going to see him after he's back to normal?"

"Why would you ask that?"

Amanda heard papers shuffling and water running in the background. All typical stalling tactics while Wendy formulated her answer.

"I just thought maybe you were attracted to this guy."

Amanda glanced over her shoulder at Derek. What she saw captivated her. He was placing cups in the cupboard.

The muscles under his shirt rippled, giving her a fascinating view of his chest as he shut the cupboard door. His bicep flexed as he picked up a pot. Her gaze went to his hands, where his long fingers gripped the handle. Amanda's mouth practically watered as she recalled the feel of those strong hands gliding over her body.

She turned her back to him, before answering. "I am attracted to him, but he's not a stray puppy. I can't keep him just because I think he's cute."

"Suit yourself, but if I were you, I think I'd figure out a way to try."

Amanda could almost see Wendy rolling her eyes and shrugging her shoulders. "I have to go. But before I do, I need you to do me a favor."

Wendy perked up. "What? Anything!"

"I need you to cancel the shows for the next couple of days."

Silence met the request. The seconds ticked by.

"Wendy?"

"You've never cancelled a show. Not even when you had walking pneumonia. Are you sure?"

Amanda sighed. "I'm positive. I am going to take Derek to his grandmother's house. I hope that seeing her will snap him out of the trance. If that doesn't work, I'm not sure what I'll do."

"He must be some kind of guy."

He is . . .

"I'll talk to you later. Bye." Amanda clicked the off button without waiting for Wendy to respond. It was a rare day when she left her assistant speechless. But Wendy was right, she'd never cancelled a show—ever. This was a first and it made her decidedly uneasy.

How could four days spent with a stranger change her life so much? She brushed the thought aside as she returned the phone to its cradle.

"I'm sorry I snapped at you. I'm just not myself lately. Are you ready to go?" Amanda asked, looking up into Derek's stormy eyes.

"Just give me a minute." Derek slipped into her bedroom. She heard the faucet running a moment later.

Last night's events flooded her memory. It had truly been the best sex of her life, but more than that, she'd actually connected with this man. He was considerate and kind, thinking of her needs along with his own. He was a giving lover. *Oh my goodness, was he a giving lover.*

She recalled his face buried between her thighs and then his shaft stretching and filling her. Amanda whimpered as her body responded to the memories. She grabbed the back of the sofa as an anchor to keep from marching into the bedroom and demanding they do it all again.

Derek appeared a few minutes later, shaven and washed. He looked so handsome standing there in his wrinkled clothes.

"I hope you don't mind, but I used your razor and a bit of your toothpaste."

Amanda shook her head. If he was any other man, she'd be outraged. "Nope, that's fine." She smiled. "Ready to go?"

"As I'm ever going to be."

Thirty minutes and four detours later, they arrived at the home of Joan Lansing, Derek's grandmother. She was a pleasant looking woman with silvery white hair. She had the same piercing gray eyes as her grandson, telling Amanda without words that nothing got past her. Her body held the padding from many years of fine cooking. She opened the screen door with a wide smile and beckoned them in.

"Nana Joan, you look well." Derek leaned in to kiss her cheek.

"I am. Now who is this fine young lady?" Her gaze spun to Amanda.

"This is Ms. Amanda Dillon. She's a celebrity of sorts," he added.

"Mustn't be much of one, I've never heard of her."

Amanda laughed at her candidness. She couldn't help it. Joan Lansing told it like it was. *How refreshing*.

Derek colored. "Just because you haven't heard of her, doesn't mean she's not a celebrity."

"Are you talking back to me?" One meaty hand went to her plump hip.

Derek's eyes widened. "No ma'am." He shook his head.

Amanda bit her lip to keep from laughing again. She hadn't missed the sparkle of affection shining in Joan's eyes when she gazed at her grandson.

"Well don't just stand there, go into the living room and have a seat. I'll be in with coffee in a moment."

Amanda reached out to stop Joan. "I'm sorry, but I don't drink coffee."

Joan smiled brightly. "Well that's a shame, dear. It looks like you'll have to today." With that, she strode off to the kitchen.

Amanda snorted. "Is she always like that?"

Derek grinned. "As I recall."

His words slapped sense into her. "Does anything seem familiar?"

"I know she's my grandmother and that I love her, but other than that . . ." He shrugged.

This couldn't be happening to her. What was she going to do now? Her gaze followed Joan's retreat into the kitchen.

"I'll meet you in the living room." Before Derek could respond, she'd strolled off, hot on his grandmother's heels.

Panic gripped Derek. He hadn't gotten a chance to warn his grandmother. He'd wanted to whisper in her ear that they needed to talk, but Amanda stood too close and would have overheard.

Now she was in the kitchen, saying God only knows

what to his grandmother, and he couldn't think of a thing to stop her. He paced in the hall a moment before growling in frustration. His steps fell heavy across the tan carpeted floor as he strode into the living room.

Modest brown leather furniture landscaped the room. Nana Joan had two sofas that faced one another with a reclining chair at one end. It had been his grandfather's favorite. Nana Joan refused to part with the chair, even though it had a rip in the seat. A gas fireplace took up the bulk of one wall, its mantel littered with photos taken of him while he was growing up.

Derek smiled when his gaze touched on the one where he sat on Nana Joan's lap. His two front teeth were missing in action, and he and Nana appeared to be having a tickle fight. All his memories of this woman and this house were joyous, full of love and laughter.

He'd learned what it was like to be a man from his grandfather Pete. The pain of his passing was still fresh in his heart, even after all these years. Derek cleared his throat. He missed him.

He turned from the mantel and sat on one of the couches. The room reminded him of everything he was missing in his life: family, kids—a wife. All things he'd managed to gloss over until he came for a visit. Now it was impossible to ignore. Not that it mattered much anymore, now that Nana was about to blow his little charade out of the water. How ironic that the one woman he could see himself settling down with was the one woman who'd soon hate his guts.

Amanda entered Joan Lansing's kitchen with one thing on her mind—Derek. As much as she'd miss him, she had to get him out of this trance. She wouldn't be able live with herself otherwise. It wasn't like she could care for him for the rest of his life, could she? The thought sent delicious possibilities zinging through her head.

Earlier to Wendy, Amanda had likened Derek to a stray

puppy. *You'd love a stray puppy if you found one, wouldn't you?* Of course, she would, but Derek wasn't a puppy, so she couldn't keep him, could she?

No!

She wanted Derek of his own free will and the only way that could happen is if she woke him up.

"Joan, I need your help."

"Yes, dear." Joan glanced up from scooping grounds into the coffeepot.

"It's a long story, but I'll try to make it short."

Joan's brow furrowed in confusion. "I'm not sure what you're talking about, dear."

"Your grandson Derek came to my show a few nights ago. I'm a hypnotist." Amanda pressed a hand to her chest, trying to still her raging heartbeat. "Anyway, he participated, which called for me to hypnotize him, and I haven't been able to wake him since."

Joan smiled and went back to scooping. With that pile of grounds, they'd probably have cappuccino.

"There's nothing wrong with my grandson," she finally said, looking up long enough to reach for a pitcher of water.

"What do you mean? I don't think you understand." Amanda sounded frantic, even to her own ears.

"No, dear, you don't understand. The only thing *wrong* with my grandson is he's crazy about you."

Amanda's mouth dropped open for a couple of beats.

"Close your mouth, dear. I don't need to see your molars," she snickered and then went to a Winnie the Pooh cookie jar and retrieved a handful of cookies. "These are Derek's favorites. He loves oatmeal cookies."

Amanda recovered. "Ma'am, I hate to contradict you, but Derek liking me is the problem."

Joan shook her head. "You young people these days make love so difficult. Back when Pete was courting me, we went to socials and held hands. When he told me he loved me, we got married." She wiped her hands on a nearby rag.

"But . . ."

"Has Derek told you he loved you yet?" she asked, picking up the tray of coffee and cookies.

"No." Amanda started. "He hasn't said that." *Was it possible he truly cared for her?* Amanda's heart leapt at the thought.

Joan smiled. "He will. He probably just hasn't had time with that big, fancy magazine job of his."

Amanda blinked. She'd obviously misunderstood Nana Joan. "What did you say?"

"I said, he will probably tell you he loves you once he has a break from that demanding job of his."

Amanda's heart slammed in her chest and then shattered. "H-He's a—a journalist," she said through clenched teeth.

"One of the best." Joan's chin tilted higher and pride shone in her eyes.

"Thank you, Nana Joan. You've been more than helpful."

"You're welcome, dear." The old woman paused. "Are you feeling well?"

"I'm fine, thanks."

But she wasn't fine. Nothing about this situation was fine. He'd lied to her. He'd pretended to be something that he wasn't. Worse still—he'd pretended to be hypnotized.

Amanda's stomach roiled. She waited for Nana Joan to leave the room, before grasping the counter for support. What was she going to do? Hurt coiled around her heart, squeezing until she thought the blood flow would cease. Angry tears moistened her eyes. She didn't know who she was angrier with, Derek or herself.

Derek had just about convinced himself everything was going to be fine until he saw Amanda's expression as she entered the living room. In that moment, he knew he'd been busted. She averted her gaze from his and refused to sit near him when he suggested she take a seat. Her knuckles were white as she gripped the coffee cup.

"Amanda, would you like a cookie?" he offered, holding the plate.

"I don't want anything from you. Forgive me, Nana Joan, but I have to go. I-I-I just have to go." Amanda stood in a rush and walked to the door.

Derek raced after her. "Amanda, we need to talk."

"You must think I'm pretty stupid right about now."

He tried to touch her, but she pushed his hands away.

"And I suppose I am."

"No, you're not."

"I hope you got a good story out of last night. Is that why you pretended to be in a trance, to get me into bed?"

Derek heard a gasp behind him. He cringed at the thought of Nana Joan overhearing their conversation, but he couldn't allow Amanda to leave in this emotional state without an explanation.

"You know I didn't make love to you in order to have a story."

"Do I?" Her chin shot up. Pain flickered in her eyes. "Then why did you?"

Derek glanced over his shoulder one more time. Nana Joan busied herself with cleaning up the dishes.

"We can't talk here."

She snorted. "Just as I thought. You'll have to let me know when the issue is due to hit the stands. Good-bye, Derek."

The finality of her words shook him to the core. He didn't want to let her go—ever. But he had no idea how he was going to convince Amanda that the moment they'd slept together everything had changed.

She pulled free from his grasp and opened the door. He watched her walk down the sidewalk until she reached the curb, her full hips swaying side to side. Pain sliced through

Derek. He willed his feet to move, go after her. Instead, he stood frozen in the doorway, his deception weighing him down.

Amanda raised her arm and hailed a cab. Within seconds, she'd been picked up and driven out of his life.

Six

The next day the phone rang at five-thirty in the morning. Amanda answered on the second ring, since she'd spent the night wide awake. Her heart sank a notch when she realized it was Wendy.

"Amanda, you are never going to believe who you have staying in your house," her frantic voice squawked.

"No one," Amanda sighed.

The silence tolled as loudly as any bell on her frazzled nerves. Several times during the night, Amanda had turned over half expecting to see Derek's smiling face, but he hadn't been there. His appearance, his act, everything had been an illusion. A con orchestrated to get him close enough to her so he could write an article.

"Derek Armstrong is a reporter for *Mode Times Magazine*. He's the reporter who's been after the interview. The same one who sent you all those flowers. I thought maybe he was faking it, but I had no idea he was a reporter."

"You what? You mean to tell me you knew he wasn't under a trance and you let me take him home with me!"

Wendy whimpered. "I wouldn't have if I'd have known who he was. I thought meeting a nice man would be good for you."

"Oh, Wendy..." Amanda didn't know how to feel. Derek was good for her in so many ways, but she couldn't get past his deception. Not that it mattered, since they wouldn't be speaking ever again.

"I'm sorry, Amanda. I truly am. If you want to fire me I'll understand."

Amanda could hear Wendy crying softly into the phone. "Fire you. Are you kidding? I wouldn't fire the best assistant I've ever had. Besides, you're my friend. You were only looking out for my best interest."

"Amanda," she hiccoughed. "I don't deserve you as a boss."

"No you don't, but I'm afraid we're stuck with each other." She laughed.

Wendy sniffled. "Funny. Real funny. So what are you going to do?"

"About?"

"You know who."

Pain sliced through Amanda, even without the mention of Derek's name. In a few short days, she'd actually fallen in love with the louse.

"There's nothing I can do. He'll probably come out with some pithy article about the *real* Amanda Dillon, telling the world about our bedroom escapades."

"So you did sleep with him! I thought so."

It must be the lack of sleep that pried Amanda's lips open enough to spill that bit of information. She supposed it didn't really matter if Wendy knew about it or not, because soon the whole world would know.

"It doesn't matter."

"Yes, it does. Do you love him?"

Amanda groaned. "Wendy, that's a stupid question, even for you."

"You didn't answer me. Do ... you ... love ... him?"

She sighed. "I thought I did, but..." She shrugged. "Can I go back to sleep now?" *Like that's going to happen.*

Wendy winced. "I'm sorry. I was so excited. I forgot what time it was. I'll let you go and call you later this afternoon."

"Sure." Whatever. It didn't matter. She'd still be sitting in the same position on the couch.

Derek Armstrong sat at his desk staring into space. He'd perused the file on Amanda's parents and now understood her reluctance to speak with the press.

Her father had been ruined by a newspaper reporter's article when she was a child. He'd been accused of bilking money from a retirement fund and was later acquitted when it was discovered the president of the company had been behind the thefts.

By then though, it had been too late for him to recover his once sterling reputation; magazines and newspapers across the country had run with the story. Randall Dillon had been labeled a thief. From what Derek could gather, he'd died a broken man, leaving his wife and daughter in dire straits.

That explained why every dime she made from the show went into a savings account for her and her mother.

Hell, no wonder Amanda didn't give interviews.

For the first time in Derek's life, he knew what heartbreak was. And he didn't like it one bit. After Amanda had left, Nana Joan had scolded him, shaming him over his deceptive behavior and for breaking the poor girl's heart. Her heart? What about his?

Had he broken Amanda's heart? Did she care enough for him to allow him to do so? Derek didn't know, but he felt as guilty as the time he'd lifted candy from the dime store and Nana Joan had made him take it back. Like then, this was a lesson he would not soon forget.

He'd been a fool. An arrogant, self-centered, asinine fool. How could he convince Amanda that he understood her pain and fear? And that he'd changed. Hell, she'd been the one to change him.

Derek considered every way of approaching Amanda. None seemed acceptable. She'd called him a liar. Perhaps he was, but he'd never lied to her about his profession. She'd just never asked what he did for a living. If she had, he would have told her.

Fingers laced behind his head, he rocked, tipping his chair back, while balancing with his foot. There had to be some way back into her life. That's what got you into trouble in the first place, his conscience warned. He ignored the warning. He was just miserable enough to be desperate.

A loud knock sounded on Amanda's door. She jumped out of her half-conscious state. What time was it? The clock over the stove blinked twelve. Someday she was going to have to figure out how to set that stupid thing.

The sound came again, only this time louder. "I'm coming." Amanda padded barefoot across the hardwood floor and unlocked the door.

"You should check to see who it is before you open the door," Derek snapped.

He looked as disheveled as she felt.

"I had a pretty good idea who it was. Besides, getting mugged wouldn't make my day any worse."

He shouldered the door, almost as if he expected her to slam it in his face.

Amanda ran a trembling hand through her tangled hair and turned to walk back into her apartment. She didn't have the energy to argue with this man. She just wanted to crawl back into bed and go to sleep for a week.

"Derek, I don't want to fight. You got what you wanted, so can't you just leave me alone."

"No."

"Why?" The question turned into a plea.

"Because I didn't get what I wanted."

His words stopped her cold.

Amanda spun, newfound anger curling in her belly and

awakening her senses. "Let me get this straight, you pretend to be in a trance, you lie to me about your identity, and then you have the nerve to come back here expecting more. Have you lost your ever-loving mind?"

Derek listened to Amanda seethe. She looked so beautiful, glowing from her anger. From her crumpled sweats to her mussed hair, it was more than obvious she hadn't slept. Her normally vibrant blue eyes were now tinged with red. Guilt swamped him. He shouldn't have deceived her by pretending to be in a trance, but he wouldn't accept responsibility for lying.

Derek shut the door behind him and locked it before turning to face Amanda. "Give me one instance where I lied to you."

Amanda's nostrils flared and she clenched her jaw. "You lied about who you were and what you did for a living."

"I never lied to you."

"You didn't tell me you were a reporter," she snapped.

"You never asked."

Derek closed the distance between them. "You've been so worried about being burned by me, you didn't stop to think that just maybe, I'd fallen for you," he said. "Damn it, I love you. Get it?"

Amanda stood in stunned silence. She hadn't asked what Derek's profession was because she'd been too concerned over the fact that he wouldn't come out of induction.

"It's probably just the trance talking," her voice squeaked out.

His gaze slid over her body and his eyes narrowed. "No, it's not the trance. I never was under and you know it. You couldn't put me under."

"I-I could too."

He smiled lethally. "Go ahead. Try."

"Sit down!"

Derek did as she commanded. Amanda retrieved her coin and went through a simple induction. When she was finished, Derek looked relaxed with his eyes closed and his breathing deep and even. His wide chest rose and fell with each exhalation.

So she couldn't induce him, eh? She just showed him.

Amanda's fingers itched to touch him one more time. Against her better judgment, she reached out to touch his chest. His heartbeat was slow and steady. Amanda smiled to herself. She was about to pull away when his eyes flew open, emotion shimmering in their gray depths. The second their gazes locked, Derek's heart rate skyrocketed.

Amanda gasped. She could feel her eyes widen as she snatched her hand back. It wasn't possible was it? Did he love her? She scrambled to her feet to get away, her heart slamming in her chest. Before she could make a clean break, Derek caught her upper arms, effectively halting her escape.

"Where do you think you're going?"

Amanda swallowed hard. "Nowhere."

"Good! Because I'm not going to let you get away so easily." His lips quirked. "Face it, Amanda, we're meant for each other."

"I don't have to face anything. The article speaks for itself."

"There's not going to be an article."

Hope bloomed in Amanda. "What do you mean?" she asked, not wanting to read too much into his statement.

Derek pulled her onto his lap. "I called my editor earlier and told him the story was a bust." He grinned. "Let's just say he didn't appreciate the three A.M. wake-up call."

"Oh . . ." she managed, before wetting her lips. Amanda's gaze locked on Derek's mouth. She wanted him to kiss her so bad. She parted her lips to ask, but needn't have bothered.

Derek's mouth descended upon hers, ravaging her lips, igniting her body. His kiss was long and drugging, his tongue sweeping into her mouth, before retreating. Minutes later, he pulled back. His breath mingled with hers, heating her skin, echoing like a cry in the silence of the apartment. He picked her up and walked the short distance to her bedroom. Instead of stopping there, he proceeded to the bathroom.

The warmth of Derek's body surrounded her, seeping into her blood, before settling in her bones. Amanda sighed. She did love this man. One night without him and she'd been miserable. It would take a while to rebuild the trust she'd automatically felt toward him, but they had a lifetime to work on it.

"I thought we could both use a shower, since it's been a long night."

"You're probably right." She shivered in anticipation.

Derek set Amanda down on the toilet and then turned on the water. He kept shoving his hand under the spray until he was satisfied that the temperature was right. Then he turned to face her and began to undress.

Amanda's mouth went dry as his shirt hit the bathroom floor. His pants followed quickly, revealing his magnificent erection. Try as she might, Amanda couldn't rip her gaze away from the pale organ with its violet crown. Derek's lips twitched in what appeared to be amusement, as pure unadulterated hunger filled his eyes.

"Care to join me?" he asked as he stepped inside her glass shower.

Steam rose in plumes as Derek leaned forward and drenched his head. Amanda stared in awe as the droplets of water cascaded over his broad shoulders, tumbling down his back, before curving decadently around the slope of his tight butt.

Her fingers trembled as she slipped her sweats down her hips. Her T-shirt followed suit as she stepped in behind Derek and closed the door. It was like stepping into the ring with a ferocious lion. He turned on her, his movements swift and controlled. His hands gripped her shoulders before sliding down her arms and around to her back.

He reached lower until he found her hips. His grip tightened and Derek spun her around, controlling her movements so she didn't slip and fall.

"Put your hands against the wall, Amanda," he whispered seductively in her ear.

Amanda whimpered, then did as he'd asked.

"Now I want you to spread your legs."

He gently kicked them apart like he was about to frisk her. Amanda's pulse quickened and her nipples throbbed painfully. The spray from the shower barely hit her, because of Derek's body blocking its force. The effect left the front of her body cool while her backside scalded.

Derek slipped his hand between her legs and played with her slick opening. She dripped and it wasn't because of the shower. He teased and circled, drawing near and then away from the bundle of nerves that ached for his touch. Her lower body strained to get nearer.

"If you move, I'll stop."

He was torturing her. Torturing her with his touch, his words, and the heat of his body at her back. Soon, she'd surrender willingly to anything.

"Derek, please," she muttered.

Amanda felt the ridge of his shaft slide between her buttocks before slipping to her needy core. She shuddered, her breath coming out in gasping pants.

Derek teased her flesh with the head of his cock, before slipping an inch inside. "You have no idea what you do to me," he said, nibbling on her ear.

"I've got a pretty good idea." Amanda glanced over her shoulder at him and smiled, before resting her forehead against the moist tile wall.

Derek thrust forward hard enough to bring Amanda to her toes, burying his shaft to the hilt inside her body. His hips bucked and rolled, plunging and spearing deep enough to feel as if he'd reached her heart.

In truth, he had.

His fingers sought and found her buried treasure, flicking

the greedy nerves with the edge of his fingernail as his hips pistoned behind her. Amanda moaned. The slap of wet skin and warm spray filtered through her senses as they made love without the lies, without the deceptions. Nothing stood between them now, but the truth.

Her body tensed as her need rose. She could feel Derek's raspy breath against her skin, then the sting of his teeth as he nipped her shoulder. One hand held her, while the other explored.

Amanda no longer inhabited her body. She mewled as her orgasm rocked her, rolling her in a spasm of endless desire. A short time later, Derek grunted behind her and followed in her wake.

They stood in the shower, bodies trembling for several minutes, until it registered that the water had turned cold. Derek slipped from Amanda and then turned to shut off the faucet.

He kissed her shoulder where he'd bitten her and then stepped out and grabbed a towel. He held it wide and waited for her to come to him. She did and he enveloped her in warmth. Derek dried Amanda as if she were made of porcelain. He rubbed her skin until not a drop of water remained, then he dried himself, his movements brisk and efficient like the man.

Exhausted, they dragged themselves back into the bedroom. Derek threw the covers back and waited for Amanda to crawl under, before following her. He pulled her next to him, tucking her into his shoulder. His hand ran over her arm as he placed feathery kisses on her brow. This felt right, they felt right. Amanda relaxed.

"So what are you going to do next, if you don't turn in a story on me?"

He shrugged. "I thought maybe we could write the story together. You'd even get final say-so."

"Really?" Amanda's eyes lit up.

"Really." He grinned, and then kissed her nose. "Don't

you know you've had me mesmerized since the first time I laid eyes on you?"

Her gaze widened in surprise. "I did?"

He kissed her cheek. "Yes," he murmured. "You did."

Amanda bit her lip. "I suppose it's only fair that we both fall under the same hypnotic spell."

Derek rolled her beneath him. The ridge of his erection teased her tender flesh until her breath caught. "Abracadabra, baby."

Here's a look at Nancy Warren's latest
romantic comedy for Brava,
TURN LEFT AT SANITY
a February 2005 release from Kensington . . .

"Don't you think we'll end up more frustrated if we keep talking and it doesn't go anywhere?"

"Well, last night would have been too soon, but now . . ."

Now, what? Joe came up with an answer for her. "Now I've passed the Miss Trevellen school of larceny and good manners?"

She laughed aloud. Out of her peripheral vision she could see that Gregory Randolph had the hood up on Joe's car. How long did this disabling business take? She was in a cold sweat, gulping her cocoa like it was courage-giving whiskey.

Greg was bent over the open hood of the car, his white T-shirt gleaming against the darkness. *Please let him get the job done quickly.*

A computerized *ping* broke the strained silence in the office and Joe said, "Ah, my e-mail."

He started to turn his chair around to his computer, which faced the window, which looked out on a man screwing with his car.

She had to stop him. No time to think. She stuck her foot out and stopped the chair mid-twirl.

"Emmylou, I need to get that," Joe said, an edge to his voice.

"But I need you," she said, hoping that her voice sounded husky with passion and not strained by panic.

He opened his mouth, no doubt to tell her to get a grip, or at least wait until he'd read his e-mail. She couldn't let that happen, so she launched herself at him, sloshing cocoa mug and all.

"Whaa—" he managed before her lips clamped over his.

Blindly she managed to get her mug onto the desktop so her hands were free, then she plunged them into his hair, making a human vise to keep his head from turning. She opened her legs around his and snugged up tight onto his lap.

It was a move born of desperation and if he pushed her off him, which she was pretty certain he'd do, she'd end up sprawled on her butt all over the rug and when he turned around, he'd view more than his e-mail.

She expected to go sailing through the air and hit the rug ass-first. She expected outrage when he caught sight of Greg out there messing with his car. What she hadn't expected was that after a startled second of total stillness, Joe would kiss her back.

Oh, not just kiss her, but make love to her mouth.

His passion exploded around her and in her, sparking her own. She nipped at his lips, grabbed the back of his head to pull him closer, felt his mouth so hungry on hers, on her skin, his hands in her hair, on her neck, racing over her back.

". . . want you," he said and the echo of those words played over and over in her head. *Want you, want you, want you . . .*

Heat began to build in the three-point triangle of nipples and crotch. If Dr. Beaver was right, she had a dandy little electrical circuit running between those three hot spots.

He moaned with hunger, or maybe that was her, hard to tell over the pounding of her heart.

He pulled at the buttons on her shirt, fumbling open the top one, and then the second, while she waited in a fever of impatience. She forgot why she was doing this, forgot everything but the fact that she needed this man and she needed him now. He got the rest of the buttons undone, not smoothly but fast, then pushed the sleeves down her arms to her wrists and stopped, so she ended up with her arms bound behind her, a circumstance he seemed to enjoy.

With some wriggling she could easily free her arms, but he looked so pleased with himself she let well enough alone.

"I like you in this posture," he explained with a devilish glint in his eyes. The fatigue had vanished and he pulsed with energy. "Your breasts thrust forward, and your busy hands still. No bread baking, flower arranging, cookie cooling. All you can do is sit there and let me touch you."

And check out Alison Kent's
sexy new thriller
THE McKENZIE ARTIFACT
available now from Kensington . . .

The drapes over his motel room's window pulled open, Eli McKenzie stood and stared through the mottled glass, squinting at the starburst shards of sunlight reflected off the windshields of the cars barreling down Highway 90 in the distance.

Second floor up meant he could see Del Rio, Texas, on the horizon, and to his left a silvery sliver of the twisting Rio Grande, a snake reminding him of the venom he'd be facing once he harnessed the guts to cross.

The room's cooling unit blew tepid air up his bare torso, making a weak attempt at drying the persistent sheet of sweat. Sweat having less to do with the heat of the day than with the choking memory of the poison he'd unknowingly ingested on his last trip here.

An accidental ingestion. A purposeful poisoning.

Someone in Mexico wanted him dead.

The only surprise there was that no one but Rabbit knew Eli's true identity. Wanting to dispose of an SG-5 operative was one thing, but he hadn't been made. Which meant this was personal.

This was about his covert identity, his posing as a member of the Spectra IT security team guarding the compound across the border.

An identity he'd lived and breathed for six months until the nausea and dysarthria, the diarrhea, ataxia and tremors turned him into a monster. One everyone around him wanted to kill.

He'd tried himself. Once.

Rabbit had stopped him and sent him back to New York and to Hank Smithson, the Smithson Group principal, to heal. Eli owed both men his life, though it was his debt to Hank that weighed heaviest.

Hank, who plucked men in need of redemption off their personal highways to hell and set them down on roads less traveled. Roads that took the SG-5 operatives places not a one of them wished to see again after reaching the end of their missions.

Places like the Spectra IT compound in Mexico.

Scratching the center of his chest, Eli shook his head and pondered his immediate future. He and Rabbit were the only ones inside the compound not working for Spectra. Outside was a different story.

And there had been one person nosing around and causing enough scenes to make a movie.

Stella Banks.

Stella Banks with her platinum blond hair and battered straw cowboy hat and legs longer than split rail fence posts. She was an enigma. A private investigator who dressed like a barrel racer and looked like a runway model.

She kept an office in Ciudad Acuna, another in Del Rio. He knew she was working the disappearance of her office manager's daughter, Carmen Garcia. The girl was fourteen, and like so many of the others gone missing recently, a beauty.

She was also currently being held inside the compound, waiting to be shipped away from her family and into a life of prostitution courtesy of Spectra IT. Or so had been the case last Eli had checked in with Rabbit.

The room wasn't getting any cooler, the day any longer,

the truth of what lay ahead any easier to swallow. Like it or not, it was time to go. Once across the border, he'd make his way south a hundred kilometers in the heap Rabbit had left parked in a field west of the city.

As much as Eli longed for a haircut and a shave, he wouldn't bother with either. The scruffy disguise went a long way to helping him blend in, to hiding the disgust he never quite wiped from his face.

Considering the condition of the car and the roads, he was looking at a good two hours of travel time. One hundred and twenty minutes to go over the plans he'd worked out with Rabbit to take down these bastards.

Plans trickier than Eli liked to deal with but which couldn't be helped. Not with the lives of twenty teenaged girls on the line.

His plans for Stella Banks he hadn't quite nailed down.

He needed her out of the way.

Before he got rid of her, however, he needed to find out what she and her outside sources could add to what Rabbit had learned on the inside.

Only then would Eli make certain she never interfered in his mission again.

He was alive.

And he was back.

That son-of-a-bitch was back.

Stella Banks curled her fingers through the chain links of the fenced enclosure and watched him leave the compound's security office and cross the yard to the barracks.

She couldn't believe it. Not after all the trouble she'd gone through—and gotten into—to get rid of his sorry kidnapping ass for good.

Next time she'd forgo the poison and use a bullet instead.

Take a sneak peek at MaryJanice Davidson's
"Ten Little Idiots," in
"WICKED" WOMEN WHODUNIT
also available now from Kensington . . .

"This is all Jeannie Desjardin's fault," Caro declared to the hallway.

Lynn Myers blinked at her. "Who—who's Jeannie Desjardin?"

"My friend. She's this awesomely horrible woman who generally revels in being bad. You know—she's one of those New York publishing types. But every once in a while she gets an attack of the guilts and tries to do something nice. Her husband and I try to talk her out of it, but . . . anyway, this was supposed to be *her* Maine getaway. But she gave me the tickets instead and stayed in New York to roast along with eight million other people." *And the yummy, luscious Steven McCord,* Caro thought rebelliously. *That lucky bitch.* "And now *look,*" she said, resisting the urge to kick the bloody candlestick. "Look at this mess. Wait until I tell her being nice backfired again."

"Well," Lynn said, blinking faster—Caro suspected it was a nervous tick—"we should—I mean . . . we should call the—the police. Right?"

Caro studied Lynn, a slender woman so tall she hunched to hide it, a woman whose darting gray eyes swam behind magnified lenses. She was the only one of the group dressed in full makeup, panty hose, and heels. She had told Caro during the first "Get Acquainted" brunch that she was a realtor from California. If so, she was the most uptight Californian Caro had ever seen. Not to mention the most uptight realtor.

"Call the police?" she asked at last. "Sure. But I think a few things might have escaped your notice."

"Like the fact that the storm's cut us off from the mainland," Todd Opitz suggested, puffing away on his eighth cigarette in fifteen minutes.

"Secondhand smoke kills," Lynn's Goth teenage daughter, Jana, sniffed. A tiny brunette with wildly curly dark hair, large dark eyes edged in kohl (making her look not unlike an edgy raccoon), and a pierced nostril. "See, Mom? I told you this would be lame."

"Jana . . ."

"And secondhand smoke *kills,*" the teen added.

"I hope so," was Todd's cold reply. He was an Ichabod Crane of a man, towering over all of them and looking down his long nose, which was often obscured by cigarette smoke. He tossed a lank section of dark blond hair out of his eyes, puffed, and added, "I really do. Go watch *Romper Room,* willya?"

"Chil*dren,*" Caro said. "Focus, please. Dana's in there holed up waiting for *les flic* to land. Meantime, who'd she kill?"

"What?" Lynn asked.

"Well, who's dead? Obviously it's not one of us. Who's missing?" Caro started counting on her fingers. "I think there's . . . what? A dozen of us, including staff? Well, four of us—five, if you count Dana—are accounted for. But there's a few of us missing."

The four of them looked around the narrow hallway, as if expecting the missing guests to pop out any second.

"Right. So, let's go see if we can find the dead person."

"Wh—why?" Lynn asked.

"Duh, Mom," Jana sniffed.

"Because they might not be dead," Caro explained patiently. "There's an old saying: 'A bloody candlestick does not a dead guy make,' or however it goes."

Jana was startled out of her sullen-teen routine. "Where the hell did *you* grow up?"

"Language, Jana. But—but the police?"

"Get it through your head," Todd said, not unkindly. "Nobody's riding to the rescue. You saw the Weather Channel . . . before the power went out, anyway. This is an island, a private island—"

"Enjoy the idyllic splendor of nature from your own solitary island off the Maine coast," Lynn quoted obediently from the brochure.

"Don't do that, it creeps me out when you do that."

"I have a photographic memory," she explained proudly.

"Congratufuckinglations. Anyway," Todd finished, lighting up yet another fresh cigarette, "the earliest the cops can get here is after the storm clears, probably sometime tomorrow morning."

"But they have helicopters—"

As if making Todd's point, a crack of lightning lit up the windows, followed by the hollow boom of thunder so loud it seemed to shake the mansion walls. The group pressed closer to each other for a brief moment and then, as if embarrassed at their unwilling intimacy, pulled back.

"They won't fly in this weather. We're stuck. Killer in the bedroom, no cops, power's out. The perfect Maine getaway," Todd added mockingly.

"It's like one of those bad horror movies," Caro commented.

"Caro's right."

"About the horror movies?"

He shook his head. "Let's go see who's dead. I mean, what's the alternative? It beats huddling in our rooms waiting for the lights to come back on, doncha think?"

"What he said," Caro said, and they started off.